I am the funny one. And I am the one who makes the plans. I'm the one who gets the invites and the vodka and keeps things on track and going all night. I know how to make Fleet McCauley laugh and how to make Nate Rosen forget his broken mirror. But all those people can turn on you so fast. I think about the way all the Sigma Chi guys cursed Number Six when he fumbled the ball, standing up, their faces red, screaming. When he was just trying his hardest to do his job, with a million people watching, a million people who will never let anything go, who will never say, "Don't worry, everything's going to be okay."

—from *Number 6 Fumbles*

number

fumbles

RACHEL SOLAR-TUTTLE

POCKET BOOKS
New York London Toronto Sydney Singapore

An *Original* Publication of MTV Books/Pocket Books

POCKET BOOKS, a division of Simon & Schuster, Inc.
1230 Avenue of the Americas, New York, NY 10020

Copyright © 2002 by Rachel Solar-Tuttle

Line from *Story of My Life* by Jay McInerney reprinted with
permission of Vintage Books

MTV Music Television and all related titles, logos, and characters are
trademarks of MTV Networks, a division of Viacom International Inc.

ISBN: 0-7434-2851-X

First MTV Books/Pocket Books trade paperback printing February 2002

10 9 8 7 6 5 4 3 2 1

POCKET and colophon are registered trademarks of Simon & Schuster, Inc.

For information regarding special discounts for bulk purchases,
please contact Simon & Schuster Special Sales at 1-800-456-6798
or business@simonandschuster.com

Cover design by Thomas Berger and Dekiah Polansky;
cover photography by Warren Darius Aftahi

Printed in the U.S.A.

For Matt, who no one would believe as a character.
You're that good.

Acknowledgments

I'd like to thank . . .

my parents, Judith and Barry, for not flinching when I left the law and when they read the racy parts, and for all the "we're proud of you"s;

A.S. and A.C., who let me run away to them;

Alice Martell, my agent, who somehow combines toughness with sweetness;

Greer Kessel Hendricks, my editor, who so gets it;

Mameve Medwed, friend, teacher, and inspiration;

Professor Al Filreis, for whom I worked really, really hard;

my patient, unpaid, informal editors (and friends);

the Red Sox—who help me dream;

and, of course, Phoebe. You know who you are.

1

★

number 6 fumbles

It's the Penn/Cornell game and we're sitting above the fifty-yard line up on the second tier with all the Sigma Chi brothers and everyone has their screwdrivers in their Hood orange-juice containers as usual and it's cold. This one player, Number Six, fumbles the ball, and I see it tumble on the field like a dropped baby and I hear the blur of the announcer and the Sigma Chi guys getting up and slapping their thighs and swearing, but what I feel is not anger but this sadness, I mean, thinking of this guy who fumbled. Were his parents watching him today? Will his girlfriend comfort him tonight? Will he try to work a calculus problem and keep thinking back to this moment?

I hear my own mother's voice from this morning's phone call: "Did you hand in the topic for your American Lit paper?" (I'm doing it on Jesse Jackson speeches and Walt Whitman poetry. How they both use repetition and rhythm—in a way that's like beating a bongo drum in the woods—to convey confidence and triumph.) "Honey, I don't think that's a good idea. Is it too late to talk to the professor?

The thing I don't think you understand is that at the college level, the expectation, in terms of scholarly . . ." Blah blah blah. I was out all night but it's this five-minute telephone conversation that has exhausted me. After I hung up on her, I put my head under the covers at the very foot of my bed. Then I screamed.

Thinking about this and about Number Six fumbling the ball suddenly makes me feel some generic negative way I can't quite pin down, except to know that I need to be somewhere else. Now. "Susan," I say, tapping her on the shoulder. She holds up one finger and freezes the smile on her face because she's in the middle of laughing at some story Fleet McCauley's telling.

"Susan, I need to go."

"Go where? To the bathroom? Eww. Wait till we get home or to the Palladium or something."

"No, just go. Get out of here."

"We could take a lap around the horseshoe, say hi to Casey and the rest of the Dekes."

"No, I mean leave. Leave the game. For good."

"What? Why? Leave the game?" Susan wrinkles her perfect nose like there's an off smell, or like she's that TV witch and can make everything normal again.

"Yeah. I just, I just have this bad feeling. I just don't want to be here."

"I don't get it, Beck. Feeling like what?"

"I don't know. Like I need to relax. Take a break or something. Get out of here."

"But we are relaxing. We are taking a break. It's a football game," Susan says.

I want to say that this is not so relaxing. Feeling bad for the guy who fumbled the ball, thinking of all the pressure he's under. And making conversation with these Sigma Chi guys is more like work

3

than fun, than unwinding. I want to lie on top of the ocean and drift, like when I was little and I noticed for the first time that the salt would make you float and you could leave the shore totally behind and just forget Solarcaine, sand in your Docksides, screaming people.

"Susan, please. When you were yakking last night under the pool table at Zete, I left with you. And I didn't give you a whole third degree. Be a friend."

"Okay. Fine. But I don't understand why we have to leave right now when the game's not even over. The band hasn't played the 'drink a toast to dear ol' Penn' song yet. I brought a whole loaf of bread so we could throw toast this time," she says, putting on her leather jacket and flipping her hair out of the collar for Fleet McCauley's benefit.

I tuck my own hair behind my ears. I always feel that my looks need tweaking. Susan and Jane and Maggie would definitely be described as pretty, or at least cute, even right when they wake up. With a little work, I can be sexy or attractive. But my hair is brown, and not a good, glamorous brown, and my eyes are set a little too deep. My features will never add up to cuteness, though in high school I once overheard my friend's brother say that I had a "teeth-gritting body."

I realize that Susan is still waiting for her answer about why we have to leave, and I guess I could leave by myself, but I'm worried that if I go off alone, I'm really going to start freaking out. If Susan and I are together, at least whatever happens will be halfway normal, because Susan's there, and Susan is the queen of normal, of doing the right thing. I can't spin out of control when I'm with Susan. "It's important. I just can't stay here anymore. C'mon, we'll go to Kelly's and get something to eat."

I like Kelly's. The food's not that great and they don't serve breakfast all day or anything, just till 3 P.M. But it's bright and crowded

4

and it's good when I don't want something more ethnic, like Indian and Thai from the trucks along the street near the classroom buildings, which is what I usually eat. So I order French toast and bacon—my usual—and we sit and wait with both of us kind of quiet, because I think we both know that something is wrong. I mean, we did just leave the game before it had even really begun. Not that we're these die-hard football fans, but we have certain rituals.

And then suddenly I just don't want to be here anymore either. Like I just can't bear to sit in this wooden chair with the artificial light shining on my empty plate for another minute. I can't even hold out for the food to come. This cheesy music-only version of some Neil Sedaka song is playing, and I take out a twenty even though the bill is nowhere near that and I put it on the table, and as I'm doing this, I'm saying how this just doesn't feel right, how I don't want to be here, and Susan's like, "Beck, can't we wait one minute? I'll get the waitress's attention and we'll ask for the check, okay?"

But I say, "No, it has to be right now. It has to be right now."

Then we're outside and we're walking up Locust Walk and she's trying to understand I know but not really, because really she's just wishing she could be back there with the Sigma Chis and flirting and showing off her boobs as usual. Susan is probably one of the worst friends I could have brought along at this moment. She has just no sense of the weirdness of things aside from maybe the Beat poetry she's reading in American Lit.

Susan says, "This is like after that Phi Delt party when we were out on the flight deck and Chandler was in from New York with his kamikaze shaker and Tasha got so wasted she gave Bunky a blow job with the door halfway open." The flight deck is not a real flight deck. It's this small, upstairs room crowded with bongs and these stolen newspaper dispensers full of Southern Comfort and

5

Tanqueray bottles. "Remember, Chandler kept saying, 'Have shaker, will travel'?"

"Susan, what are you talking about?"

"Remember," she says, arching her groomed brows and opening her eyes really wide, like of course I should know what she's talking about, "how afterwards, at like four in the morning, you suddenly decided you couldn't stand having a gray metal bedframe one more night and you were in your bra and underwear painting it white when Jane walked in with that Deke guy and he thought you were insane?"

Yeah, I remember. Half of Deke still calls me College Pro. They yell it out every time I walk into a party, like Norm on *Cheers*. "It's just like that, Susan," I say. I think: I am seriously afraid, and you're comparing it to drunken redecorating. But I don't say anything else.

So we're outside with the wind kind of pushing our butts down the slopey part of the Walk and I know she's wondering where we're going next and when I'll snap out of it and I'm trying to remember this Aretha Franklin song that's in my head but it's not "Respect." Susan doesn't know. I tell her she really should go back and she's all pseudo-concerned, which is fine, I don't expect more and I can't say for sure that I'd be different if one of my friends was acting all weird and I couldn't understand it and really wanted to be up there in the stands with some cute blond lacrosse players from Grosse Pointe. Well, yeah, actually, I know I would be different.

And I think back to just last week when Phoebe and Chevs broke up. It was 3:30 A.M. and we had all just come home for the night. No one ever says it, but Susan, Jane, and I sometimes vie for who can be the last one home. When I've come in and no one's been there but Maggie, I've run back across the street to Sigma Chi to do shots or something, just to not be the first one back. That night the three of us had been at the same party. Susan had been standing on a keg screaming, "This is the most fun I've ever had!"

Maggie was sound asleep as usual. Susan, Jane, and I were playing the Go-Go's in the living room and dancing and eating some leftover General Gau's chicken from Beijing with our fingers (Jane must have been really wasted; normally she ate only three foods: rice, steamed broccoli, and microwave popcorn) when we heard someone pounding on the door. Susan didn't want to answer it because she had been totally teasing this brother at the party earlier and she was afraid he'd followed her home. Guys did that sort of thing with Susan. So I answered the door. It was Phoebe.

Her mascara had fallen to her cheeks. "Oh my God," Jane said. "Are you all right?" Jane is generally not too quick on the uptake. Susan gave me a look. We'd both figured out what had happened. At that hour, after going to a formal with your long-term boyfriend, there aren't that many reasons why you'd be crying at your best friend's door.

"What can we do?" Susan asked.

"Can I talk to Beck? Do you guys mind?"

Susan and Jane shook their heads. "Let's go to my room," I said. I have a single this semester.

I handed Phoebe the tissue box and tapped a cigarette out of my pack for her. Her fingers shook as she reached for it. I lit it and one for me and cracked the window. My roommates don't like it when I smoke in the apartment. They only smoke in bars. Phoebe blew her nose hard. "It was like, one minute we're talking and the next minute we're broken up."

"Start at the beginning. Something happened at the semiformal tonight?" I rubbed her back.

"Yeah. You know, he was basically ignoring me the whole time. But everyone was toasting us and saying how great we were together

7

and everything. So I didn't think anything of it. I was like, whatever, he wants to get wasted with his brothers, no biggie.

"And then we went back to my place and he was pissed because he lost his Ralph Lauren gloves somewhere. And that's all he could talk about. And so finally I said, 'What is going on here?' and he said, 'I'm looking for my fucking gloves!'"

"That's so obnoxious."

"And then he's like, 'Look, it's not just that. I just don't think this is working out,' and I totally froze. Thank God, because that's the only thing that kept me from bursting into tears right there. And I tried to have a shred of dignity and not ask why, not be begging or anything, but then I totally broke down. Shit, we were together almost a year!"

Why were they all so predictable? We are always looking for these diamonds in the rough, and it seems like in the end all they ever are is rough. "That's so natural, Phoebe. You deserve an explanation."

"Yeah. So he just said he wasn't sure."

"He wasn't sure?" Asshole. He was sure when he was sleeping with her. When did this supposed confusion set in? I pictured myself storming down the darkened Walk in my pajamas, finding him, punching him in his phony smiling face. "No one fucks with Phoebe," I'd say.

"He said he wasn't sure and he had never been sure exactly, about us, and now it was becoming this really big thing. So that was his reason."

"What a schmuck! We can make his life a living hell. Totally. We'll have *34th Street* print that he has an STD." I crushed my cigarette out so hard I sent sparks flying onto the carpet.

Phoebe laughed and reached for another tissue. "Beck, the thing is, I did everything you're supposed to do. I was casual. I gave

8

him space. I didn't ask questions. Like 'Where is this going?' or whatever. He had to have his precious Sunday-night ritual, watching fucking *Married With Children* at Abner's and eating cheese steaks with that schmo from the squash team. I never said a word. He did all that stuff with the brothers. We went out alone maybe one night a month. God, I fucking baked him cookies during his hell week!"

Jane knocked on the door. "You guys all right?" she asked. Then she stood just inside the doorway. Jane has a way of lingering like that, popping up and just sticking around. Especially when there's turmoil involved.

"Uh-huh," Phoebe sniffled. Then she said suddenly, "My God, remember how he didn't want to have sex for so long and he was so weird about it? Well, I guess that's because he wasn't sure about us. At least he tried to be noble or whatever. I should have known."

"But you did eventually?" Jane asked. "Or did you just—" I shot her a shut-up look.

Phoebe rolled her eyes. "Well, duh, yeah, we did eventually. Who else but Tasha just does that anymore?" We all laughed. Tasha believes in remaining "technically" a virgin until marriage, or very deep love, or something.

"Phoebe, I think Susan and I are going to go to sleep," Jane said. "Are you going to be all right?"

Of course not, I thought. She's going to remember this night forever. She's going to replay every micromoment in her head a million times and wonder what she could have done differently, if Chevs was her destiny and she just screwed it up somehow.

"I'm okay," Phoebe said. I could see that she just wanted to get rid of Jane. "Totally. Go ahead."

Jane closed the door.

"If you want to stay here, you can use my sleeping bag," I said.

9

"Yeah, actually that would be really good. Thanks." We pushed my clothes aside and rolled out the sleeping bag. "I miss him already, Beck. Even though he's such a jerk. It's so frustrating, because—because I thought it was good. I really did. And I can't hate him." She wiped her eyes and tried to smile. "He made me French toast one morning and he put cinnamon in the batter. Cinnamon in the batter!"

"You're going to be fine. Someone else will put cinnamon in the batter. I swear. Try to get some rest. Wake me if you can't sleep. And if you can't deal with class tomorrow, we'll stay here and eat Roy Rogers and watch soaps all day."

"Earth to Beck," Susan says. "You're not talking."
"I know," I say.

2

★

i am not a plant

I tell Susan to go back to the game, because I'm starting to feel like I just need to be alone, and eventually she does. Though I'm glad, in a way I'm also sad as soon as she disappears over the hill, because I feel this loneliness so strong and so sudden it makes my throat ache. I go down to the Uni-Mart and buy Parliaments and a package of Twizzlers and a box of Kraft macaroni and cheese. We live in these pseudo-apartments called the high-rises, which are on campus so you have to show your ID to get in, but which are set up like real apartments: living room, kitchen area, two singles and a double. This is where most sophomores live. We're a step up from the freshman quad but not yet ready to change our own lightbulbs.

I go to the window and open it—halfway because the windows can't open all the way due to the suicide risk—and start packing the cigarettes against the pouchy part of my palm. I like this rhythmic motion; it satisfies me for a while. I also like looking forward to things: the macaroni, the cigarette after the meal, the Twizzlers. It comforts me to think these things all lie ahead, this little path of pleasures.

That's one of the most enjoyable aspects of smoking, the knowledge that for those few minutes it takes you to smoke that cigarette there's nothing else you have to do. I never stub out a cigarette halfway.

I think about the night before, how just one night ago, I was happy. I'd gotten us invites to Sigma Chi from my friend from home, Nate Rosen. Before the party started, I'd taken Nate with me for protection and gone to the liquor store over on Forty-second for a fifth of Bankers. "See ya tonight, kid," he'd said, winking at me, before leaving me on the walk, halfway between Sigma Chi and the high-rises. I called Phoebe and we got ready together and drank shots and danced around to Madonna before the party.

There was a huge line at Sigma Chi, so we held hands and squeezed to the front. Only freshmen wait in line. We saw Nate just inside the door. "Nate, Nate!" I said. He told the bouncer, a big pledge from Long Island that they called Plane, since he's "a simple tool," to let us in.

Inside, I took out my flask and rummaged through the Sigma Chi kitchen until I found an econo-vat of no-name orange juice. We went down to the basement and drank shots and sat on the window ledge singing the fight song for some reason with a bunch of brothers. Then we all danced like crazy until we were too hot to keep going. Phoebe and I found Nate on the way to his room with two of the other brothers who wanted some soh coh from his fridge.

We went up with them. We sat on their loft listening to Bob Marley. Sigma Chi was having a rodent problem and there was a picture of a mouse on the wall and a scoreboard marked "us" and "them" with hatch marks. So far, the mice were winning. Reece Chapin and Fleet McCauley were chewing tobacco and spitting into a giant jar labeled Dutch Pretzels that someone's mother had sent. Nate put on this Led Zeppelin tape, which Phoebe and I hate, except for "Fool in the Rain." Fleet lay down on the floor and started measuring everything using his body and announcing that the hallway was "one Fleet wide" and the bed was "one point five Fleet units long." "Fool in the Rain" came on, and Nate started swinging on a beam and a bunch of us were jumping on the bed, hard. Somehow all the bouncing toppled Nate's mirror, which smashed into a million pieces, and we all moved to shield our eyes.

"Shit," Nate said.

"Stay calm," I said. I froze where I stood and then jumped off the bed. "Just a little party foul. C'mon, we'll go to Troy's."

Nate kept looking at his blue bedspread, which sparkled with glass shards like an Indian pillow.

"C'mon, Nate." I grabbed his hand and led him away. "I'll treat you to eggles."

"Two eggles? And gravy cheese fries?" He started to grin.

"Absolutely." It was important that the broken mirror not be a buzz kill. I hustled everyone out. Downstairs the house had almost emptied. Jane was sitting on the steps talking to a cute pledge I knew had a girlfriend. We skidded into the night singing "Fool in the Rain." Nate put his arm around me. "Kid, you are so much fun. I'm always crazy when I'm with you," he said.

Troy's was packed, but Sigma Chi has kind of a reserved seat in one corner, next to the rubber plant. We banged our forks on the plastic, checkered tablecloth in time to "Fool in the Rain," which was still in our heads, and everyone laughed when Nate used my head as a drum and I smacked him back. Then everyone dug into eggles and gravy cheese fries and Cokes until we all felt sick. Afterward, we went back to this off-campus house where they had a twelve-man Jacuzzi, and someone had a video camera, and we all jumped in with our clothes on, and this woman who I recognized as the editor of the women's literary magazine or some other feminist organization was getting caught on tape in wet, white cotton underwear, talking about what great guys the Sigma Chis are. "Do you know you're being filmed?" Phoebe asked.

"Isn't it great?" Ms. Editor said.

Phoebe and I fell asleep on the couch where we'd laid ourselves out to dry. We woke up at six and ran back to the high-rises.

Sometimes I wake up and don't know where I am. Sometimes when I'm not even sleeping. I'll just be in the middle of things, and everyone is laughing, and I'll just look up for a second and think, "How did I get here?" but then I'll have a drink, or dance harder, and just re-lose myself. I am supposed to be the fun one. I'm the one who keeps the buzz going. But I don't know how I got here. It's like I got on a roll at some point and never stopped. Sometimes I can't even believe I ended up at Penn. When I think back to the admissions process, the whole thing seems unreal.

"I'll never put a Barnard sticker on my car," my father said as we walked onto the campus for my first college interview.

"Oh, David," my mother sighed.

"No, Dad? What school would be good enough to rate a sticker on the Porsche?"

"Of the schools you're applying to? Only Penn," he said. We continued to walk in silence. Then, as I pushed open the heavy door to the admissions office, he added, "On second thought, not even a Penn sticker. It'd ruin the line of the car. Maybe on your mother's. Not Barnard though. Or Vassar or Trinity, either."

In my interview, the woman said, "We like to think of Barnard as a series of concentric circles. There's Barnard. And then there's Barnard and Columbia. And then there's Barnard, Columbia, and Morningside Heights. And then there's Barnard, Columbia, Morningside Heights and . . . and . . . ?" She waited for me to fill in the blank.

My eyes lingered on some chickadees on the windowsill out-side as I dreamed of my father's car, plastered with U. Mass. stickers. I willed myself to attention. "And New York?"

"Yes!" She sounded so excited I thought she'd leap up and hug me.

Then, after she explained all about Barnard's connection with, yet superiority to, Columbia, she suddenly asked me about bowls.

"Excuse me?"

"If you could have a gold bowl or a wooden bowl, which bowl would you have?"

"A wooden bowl," I said instantly.

"Interesting. And why is that?"

"Because salad would taste very tinny and metallic in a gold bowl, I think."

She smiled. "Ms. Lowe, do people always tell you that you have an excellent sense of humor?"

"My therapist says it's an escape mechanism. I use it to diffuse the pressure. Almost like drugs."

I am the funny one. And I am the one who makes the plans. I'm the one who gets the invites and the vodka and keeps things on track and going all night. I know how to make Fleet McCauley laugh and how to make Nate Rosen forget his broken mirror. But all those people can turn on you so fast. I think about the way all the Sigma Chi guys cursed Number Six when he fumbled the ball, standing up, their faces red, screaming. When he was just trying his hardest to do his job, with a million people watching, a million people who will never let anything go, who will never say, "Don't worry, everything's going to be okay."

When my roommates come home from the game and the after parties and whatever, I'm watching *Ferris Bueller's Day Off* in the liv-ing room, but as background only; I'm mostly smoking and thinking.

16

My roommates all are so loud, compared to the silence before, talking about the game and who's hooking up with who. Maggie and Jane look meaningfully at Susan and then at me. She just had to tell them about how I freaked out. "Beck, what have you been doing all this time?" Maggie asks.

"Calm down. I'm fine. Watching a movie. Having a snack." As if a person could not possibly want to do anything besides sit above the fifty-yard line with the Sigma Chis. They both look at Susan again.

"We're worried," Jane says.

But they're not really worried about me, about whatever's dark and inside my head. They're worried about their routine, wondering when they can stop being worried and go back to the way things were before. "Well, don't be. I'm fine. I just didn't want to be at the game." I watch Ferris dance on the float in the middle of Chicago, singing "Twist and Shout."

"But you go to every game," Jane says.

"Well, maybe I got tired of it." I must sound pissed because they look at each other again and then walk out and leave me alone.

I've made the wall above my pillow into a quote board, writing lines from books and stuff in pencil. I put my favorite quotes there, like the last line from *Story of My Life* by Jay McInerney: "I'd love to think that ninety percent of it was just dreaming." Once I heard Jay McInerney read at Borders downtown, and I blurted out that I had this wall. He autographed my book, "To Rebecca—keep the wall going." Now I put up Ferris's last line, even though I haven't gotten to it yet: "Life moves pretty fast. You don't stop and look around once in a while, you could miss it." *Ferris* gives me comfort and inspiration. It makes me imagine that I could always take a day off. Phoebe's movie is *Close Encounters*. But I don't like anything about space or the surreal, anything that requires "suspending your disbelief." I pretty much thrive on my disbelief.

I decide to find an empty classroom in Steinberg-Deitrich, the Wharton building that stays open 24/7, and try to get a clue about this math class I'm in but haven't been paying much attention to. The midterm's in less than a week. Penn has these really stringent requirements about what courses you have to take, one course in this column in the course book, one in that one. And there's nothing even remotely feasible in the math column except this one class called Ideas in Math, which was supposed to be a gut. But isn't "ideas in math" an oxymoron? I always think of math as the death of ideas. I put on a little Carmex and a little mascara and some better-fitting jeans because you never know who might be at S-D, though I expect most people I know will be at after parties. I press my lips together to distribute the Carmex and resolve to be satisfied.

And I have this feeling of purpose again because I've decided that I'm just going to do one problem and I'm not going to be afraid or look for a shortcut, I'll just take it step by step, which satisfies me just thinking about it. The best places to sit at S-D are the big teacher's desks at the front of each room so you can spread out, line up your highlighters and whatever. I room-hop until I find an empty one, and then I open up a fresh pack of yellow fine-point highlighters, which have a little window in the barrel so you can see the ink running down, and click my mechanical pencil a few times to get a good point.

I start trying to do this problem where you're supposed to make a triangle out of paper, which I do, and I concentrate hard and draw the lines in pencil and use a protractor. But then the problem has so many parts, like (a) through (j), and I also realize that I really needed to have paid more attention in class. I know I'm about to cry. I have such a déjà vu feeling because this is exactly what I used to be like in high school with algebra, when I'd be doing a problem and I'd suddenly realize that it wasn't that I didn't want to do it but it was like trying to read in another language I didn't even know. Period. I used to throw a book against the wall and have to go outside and walk around or get in my mother's car and just drive down the block and I didn't even have my license.

Here I am a sophomore at an Ivy League school incapable of doing some triangle problem in a class commonly referred to as math for plants. I rip up the perfect little triangle and throw it, which is like trying to throw a potato chip, and then I slam my books into my bag and run out of the classroom and up the stairs to the door to the outside, which is heavy and metal and clangs so satisfyingly as I thrust it open and the tears start to drip into my collar.

Outside there are these benches with these grape-arbor sort of vines that creep above them. I sit there and then a laugh actually escapes, because it's almost funny, how I just feel so horrible, how I'm like this cliché fall-apart girl crying under the vines, and it's like watching it in a movie, and I can imagine the way the sound track would be all bluesy and noticeable in the quiet. It's like the feeling when you're at a party and you don't even know you're not having a good time, but then you go to pee and as soon as you crouch above the toilet, you realize that you just don't want to go out there again.

3

i never

At the very end of summer, when we first came back to school for the year, my friends and I made a sophomore pact. We were basically sick of hooking up with the same few guys at school, and we decided that this year, we were going to do something about it. Some people say "hooking up" and mean, like, actual sex, but I don't, since I hadn't even had sex at that point. I'm not a prude or morally opposed to it or anything. When I was in high school, I just thought everything would be so fumbling and ridiculous. Like where would I even do it? In a car or on a twin bed hoping someone's parents didn't come home? And I suppose I wanted to at least be somewhat into the guy, and in high school, I never was. Mostly, I tuned out the guys I dated, just nodded away while they babbled on about a lacrosse game or their new Acura.

So, as part of the pact, we all went out to this bar, New Deck Tavern, where supposedly these law school guys hang out. I dressed in my "hope I meet someone" outfit: pink cashmere sweater, gray wool shorts, little heels, and a liberal spray of Anais Anais. My friends and I are divided on the issue of shaving. Some of us regularly shave our legs, even in winter. The rest think that's a jinx: if you shave them, you'll never hook up that night. I shave. Forget superstition. You have to have hope.

A group of us were sitting at the table, looking around, waiting for interesting people, and/or law school students, to show up, and we started playing I Never, which is where one person says I never did cocaine, for example, and then everyone who has tried coke has to drink. So I said I never had anal sex, and this little Tri Delt, Rena, actually drank. I was stunned. Here I am never having had plain old missionary-type sex and this little Holly Hobbie . . . She said it started as an accident.

Maybe it was that and maybe it was also the vodka shots, but somehow I felt a sudden surge of take-no-prisoners courage. I saw these two really good-looking guys walk in; this one in particular, he was about six feet five with broad shoulders and he wore these big Timberlands and a brown corduroy shirt. So I just walked right up to him, and I was like, "I'm Rebecca Lowe and you are . . . ?" I think my voice was shaking a little. I sucked my drink hard through the tiny red straw.

He said, "Ryan Weiss," and laughed, but not in a rude way. Just to acknowledge that bold, socially inappropriate acts are a rare thing at this school. I had to admit it was funny the way I'd beelined across the room, standing and leaving my friends midsentence. He had a nice smile with a lot of teeth.

"What kind of a name is Ryan Weiss?" I asked.

"Meaning?"

"That *Weiss* sounds Jewish."

"It is."

"So what kind of a name is *Ryan* for a Jewish boy?"

"Jeez, don't hold back or anything," he said. "I know, I hate it. My middle name is Joshua. I don't know what they were thinking."

23

I can't imagine hating your own name. I like mine so much I always think that I'll definitely keep it, as is, even when I get married. "What year are you? I've never seen you before." I felt like I could pretty much say anything at this point.

"Wow, I must not exist if you've never seen me before. Hel-lo, it's like a school of twenty thousand people. What year are you?"

"I'm a sophomore. And by the way, nice attitude, Mr. Snide Remark."

"I'm a sophomore too. And you're quite the little interrogator."

Little interrogator? I think not. Actually, I'm five feet five and three-quarters, which is an above average height for the American woman." I was happy to show this off. When I'd hit five feet two, my mother had said there was no way I'd grow another inch. I willed my eyes to stop scanning him up and down. *You are so fucking hot.* "No need to insult me just because you're, like, freaky basketball-player tall."

"Thanks."

"And I'll also be needing a transcript, a recent tax return—"

"And a naked, eight-by-ten glossy," Ryan added.

"Eww. You wish!"

Ryan's friend, still standing there, cleared his throat and stuck his hand out the same way I had. *"Hel-lo!* Jared, if you care." He walked off shaking his head.

"What happened to Jared If You Care?" I asked Ryan, smiling.

"You've wounded him. Probably for life. He's making a call to his shrink back home. Or he went to the bar."

"Cute," I said, smiling, but carefully. I remembered that when I smile too big my eyes look small. And I don't like my gums.

"Apparently you think so."

"Fuck you!" I laughed and punched his arm. "It wasn't your looks. I figured you were a law student. I was looking for a meal ticket."

"Oh, so you're not shallow. Whew. Sorry to burst your bubble.

Fortunately I'm independently wealthy, though. What are you drinking?"

"A vodka grapefruit," which is mostly all I ever drink except for the vodka shots. He went to buy me another one. "And a shot too," I yelled to his back. Just my luck I go to a law school bar and meet the only sophomore there. It wasn't strange that I had never met him before; he said he wasn't in a fraternity. "So, what are you doing at New Deck, of all places?" I asked when he came back with the drinks. "We know why I'm here."

"Just sick of the bars around campus. Thought I'd try something new."

"Oh, our little bars aren't up to your standards?"

"Backstreets is okay."

I must have had a blank look.

"You've never been to Backstreets? Now that's a bar," Ryan said, looking wistful. "A real hole-in-the-wall. Games and stuff. But Jared's sick of it. This is his pick. Are we going to do these, or what?" He'd bought himself a shot too. But a brown, syrupy one.

"Soh coh?" I asked.

He nodded, knocked his shot glass against mine, and drank it down with a loud smack. The vodka made my chest burn. I winced a little.

We danced, just because we were standing on the edge of the dance floor, holding our drinks at our sides, and then we sat down at my table. I introduced him to my friends, who gave each other the eye while they checked him out. They continued their conversation as if he weren't there, planning what bar they'd go to next. Meanwhile, I became very involved in all the banter with Ryan.

"Beck. Beck. *Beck!*" Rena, the Tri Delt, finally said, interrupting us midjoke. I looked up as little as I could. "We're going to Murph's." Murph's is this bar back on the other end of campus where we go for sky labs, these drinks you can only buy in pitchers that basically have every kind of alcohol imaginable in them. When you leave for the night, Murph always says, "See ya in church," meaning back at Murph's.

I looked at Ryan, screwed up my courage again (it was easier after the shot), and said, "If I stay here instead of going to Murph's with my friends, are you going to entertain me?"

"Yeah, I'll do my best," he said.

So I waved them off.

"Suit yourself," Rena said, shaking her head, and they filed out. My ride was gone.

The prospect of being all alone with Ryan, the night all rolled out, uncertain, in front of us, made me scared, but in a good way. My fingertips were tingling. "I'm going downstairs to get cigarettes," I said. "I'll be right back."

"Get Camels," he called on my way down. I liked that he smoked too; I get sick of hearing some guy who's polluting his own liver giving me shit about smoking. But I came back up with Parliaments anyway. They're what I've smoked since high school. I like the two shades of blue on the package. He lit my cigarette off the match first, then his.

"Cool cigarettes," he mocked.

"They are cool, loser." I punched his arm. Muscular. I almost wanted to stop and just hold on.

"If you're, like, a mom."

"Hey, forgive me for starting my own trend instead of jumping on the Camel bandwagon like every other first-time smoker."

"Ouch. You're pretty cold for someone who just stalked me."

"You're going to have to get over yourself on that one, okay?" I patted his hand with mine. Then he closed his own hand over it and held it there. We did another shot together, and he started lining up the empty glasses, but I signaled the waitress to take them away. I don't like to see. Then Jared came up from the pool room. Ryan slid

26

his hand from mine and moved it to my knee under the table, rubbing circles with his thumb and forefinger. It was hard not to look. I wanted to see what such a definitive move looked like. I wanted to watch him maneuvering things to the next level. My palms got hot. This is always the best part, before, when something is sure but hasn't happened yet. I wanted to make it last.

"I'm heading out, man," Jared said.

"Jared, I want you to know that I really do care," I said, mock serious.

"Whatever." He smiled, raising his eyebrows at Ryan.

"Later," said Ryan. They did an intricate handshake.

Then I looked at Ryan, because we were really all alone now. I sipped my drink, trying not to finish another one right away. The DJ played "You Shook Me All Night Long." I like that song; the line about "knockin' me out with those American thighs" makes me feel good, that a guy would celebrate American thighs. I told Ryan how this black woman who manages the Benetton on campus always says, "Only a dog wants a bone, girl," when I complain about not being a size four anymore. He laughed.

Then "Just Like Heaven" played and I had to dance again. I always go crazy when I hear that song. I had to drag Ryan back out on the dance floor. I spun my hair around, twisted my hands above my head, swung my hips. Scott Childs always says I dance like I'm in my own living room. Ryan seemed to have excellent rhythm, in a not-trying-too-hard way. While we danced, I looked down into my drink, or at the dartboard just past his shoulder. I just couldn't look at him. Every time his eyes entered my line of vision I felt a twinge of panic, and something else. Something very, very good, uncertainness and possibilities. I stumbled a few times, and he reached out and kind of supported me. I was getting extremely buzzed.

"So where do you live?" Ryan asked.

"Why, do you think you're going there?"

"Well, I thought I would walk you home, since it's after last call and the bar's about to close. But if you want, I could put a bottle of Jack in your hand and leave you slumped in the alley instead."

"Ha, ha. I can't believe you're not in a fraternity."

"Because of my magnetic personality?"

"Because you're such an asshole."

"You're a very funny girl, you know that? I like you." He moved my face so I would have to look at him. My stomach plummeted like an elevator with cut cords. I felt my ears going explosion red.

"You're probably, like, a total genius, aren't you?" he said.

"Yep. Straight A's. And Jewish too. Your parents' wet dream." *Shut up, Beck!*

He laughed. "My mother's dream. I don't talk to my father. They're divorced. You might know his new girlfriend; I think she's a Tri Delt."

"Ouch. I'm sorry. That sucks."

"Not if you're my little sister and you want someone to share cardigans with." He held out his arm. "I would totally like to see you again."

I linked my arm into his. It was nice that he was wanting to see me again when he was still in the middle of seeing me this time. Then he walked me back to the high-rises and we laughed a lot; I could feel the alcohol kicking in a little more than I had expected. He just automatically came up to my door, which was fine except as soon as we got there, I realized that I had forgotten my keys.

Naturally, Jane and Susan weren't home; it was barely after two. Maggie was probably asleep on a stack of finance and accounting books. We banged on the door and called her name, but she didn't answer. So we sat in the concrete, gray, sort-of-puke-smelling stair-well under a flickering fluorescent light and started fooling around. At first we were just kissing for a long time, and then he pushed my bra

28

up. Which was okay. But when he started actually unhooking it, I stopped him. "No, don't," I whispered, kissing him again.

"Because you're not ready, or . . . ?"

"Because I don't want to get naked in a stairwell!" I gestured at the cinder-block walls.

"Okay." He didn't try again. In a sense I was relieved because it saved me that decision about where to stop. On the other hand, I kind of wanted something more. I wanted to wake up with him.

"We could go to your high-rise," I said.

"Uh . . . no. We can't. I have this psychotic roommate, Mondavi."

"Psychotic roommate?"

"Yeah. He throws furniture."

"Like, regularly?"

"Well, you know, like if we bring girls home or if he runs out of graph paper or something."

"You bring girls home often?" As soon as I said it, I regretted it.

He looked at me and took my hand. "No, Rebecca, I do not bring girls home often. Okay?" His tone of voice made me feel even more ridiculous. "I'll stay with you until your roommates come home."

"It's okay. I'm sure it'll only be a few more minutes, and I really don't want them coming home and finding me in the stairwell with you." My roommates would never let me live down something like that.

"Don't be ridiculous. I'm not going to just leave you here."

"No, I'm serious. I want you to. They'll be home in, like, five minutes, definitely. There's nothing going on tonight and it's after three."

"Are you sure? Why don't I just stay a few more minutes, then."

"No, I'm sure. Seriously. Go ahead." I liked that he was looking out for me.

"Well, can I get your number?"

I looked around as if a pen and paper might appear. Then I rolled up his sleeve and wrote it on his arm in my lipstick.

29

"So do you want to do something?" he asked, looking at his arm and laughing.

"Yeah. Sure. When?"

"I don't know, like tomorrow, after classes, whatever you want. I have a car. Dad's guilt gift."

Not many people at Penn have cars. It was kind of a glamorous thing. I thought of all the places I could go in a car.

"We could go down to South Street. Walk around. Get a drink and a cheese steak or something."

"A slushy drink from Fat Tuesdays?" I asked.

"Absolutely. I'll call you."

Even though I knew better, I was already envisioning being picked up at the train station after Christmas break. I always wanted someone to be waiting there for me, putting his arms around me at the station and slipping my bag onto his shoulder automatically. I watched him walk away, then fell asleep, dreaming of how his shoulders would make me feel small and safe.

I woke up in the morning, still on the stairwell and bruised from sleeping there all night. The first thing I did when I got inside was look him up in the face book. Wehr. Weis. Weld. He wasn't there. I wondered if he had lied about going to Penn; maybe he went to Temple or Drexel or something. Or maybe his name wasn't Ryan Weiss. Or maybe he'd lied about his age. In which case, he would have to be younger, or why lie? He'd have to be a freshman. It didn't make sense that he'd lie about one year, but still, I flipped madly through the face book. I could hear my heart doing that thunk thunk thunk like right before an exam. Holy shit. Class of '93. It was true.

A freshman. It wasn't that the one-year age difference was such a big deal. It was that he was a freshman. He was trying to be cool, sowing his wild oats, looking to get invites to parties, traveling n packs, eating at the dining hall. Here I envisioned him somehow making things okay, looking out for me, when he didn't even know anything himself. And also he lied to me. What else had he lied about? Did he think I wouldn't find out? Or maybe he didn't care, which I really didn't want to even consider. But that seemed like the most reasonable explanation by far, that it just didn't matter, since he'd never see me again.

"So call him," Phoebe said after a week had gone by and I'd heard nothing. It was a Sunday afternoon, and we were at her high-rise making plans for the day. Phoebe's place looks just like mine: orange-brown carpet, fake-wood table, beanbag chair from Urban Outfitters. We were sitting on the floor of her living room polishing off a big bag of Sour Patch Kids.

"Yeah, right. He lies to me and I call him. How pathetic is that?"

"Maybe he's embarrassed. He's a freshman. And he probably knows you know."

"And he should be embarrassed! He lied to me! He probably thought he'd never see me again. He probably never wants to see me again."

"Look, it's definitely going out on a limb. If you don't do it, I don't blame you. But if you want to call him, I totally think you should. You're always going to wonder, Beck. What's the worst that can happen? Act like it's no big deal. If you want to, call him while you're here."

So I did.

By the third ring, I was sweating. I shifted the phone to my shoulder and handed my cardigan off to Phoebe.

"Hello?"

I knew it was him right away but I couldn't deal. "Is Ryan there?"

"Speaking."

"Hi. It's Rebecca. Rebecca Lowe, from—"

"Yeah, what's up?"

31

I couldn't believe he was making it so fucking hard for me. No apology, no attempt at conversation. Asshole. But I couldn't back out now. And I still wanted to see him again.

"Not much. I was thinking of dropping by Smokes tonight and I thought you might want to come along."

"Smokes? I don't know . . . well, okay, whatever. Yeah, I'll come."

"Whatever?" I said. *Jerk.*

"Yeah, what time?"

"Ten-thirty. You can pick me up. You do remember where I live, don't you?"

"Yeah, I remember." I thought I detected a hint of a chuckle.

I immediately ran home to shower. I deep-conditioned my hair and used my honey bath gel. Afterward, I wrapped myself in towels and sat around the apartment, drinking cocktails and smoking, watching the clock. At ten-fifteen, I spritzed myself with Anais Anais and put on my best jeans and a soft, cream-colored sweater and laced up my black boots. When Ryan showed up at eleven-twenty, I was already buzzed, and my roommates were stalling on their way out to the Palladium. They had been fully apprised of the situation. As Ryan walked in, they finally made their way out, jingling their keys in their pockets and chanting, "Faaaace book, faaace book." It was the one time I didn't mind the way we rode each other in front of dates. He deserved it.

It upset me that Ryan looked even better than I'd remembered. As he stood in my little living room, where his body filled up most of the door frame, in a flannel shirt and jeans, I felt like he was Kryptonite draining all the superhuman resolve I had mustered.

"So," he said, pushing a lock of dark hair out of his eyes and sticking his hands in his pockets.

"So, umm, do you want to leave?" I started flipping through the coats in our coat closet, checking the pockets for my keys.

He put a firm hand on my arm and pulled me out of the closet. "So, I think there's something I should tell you."

"I think there's something I already know."

"I'm sorry. I shouldn't have done that," he said.

"So why did you?"

"Because, think about it, you were Miss Confident at New Deck, coming up to me. And you told me outright how you were looking for law school guys. What was I supposed to do? At the time I said it I didn't think we'd spend, like, all that time together."

"Why didn't you call?"

"Because I didn't know what to say to you. Because I was embarrassed. But I was glad you called me."

"You sure didn't sound like it."

"It was awkward. And I felt like an ass for not calling myself. But I was happy to hear from you, okay?"

I believed him. Actually, I felt stupid for not calling sooner, and for having just the hang-ups about freshmen that he thought I'd have. I believed that I was the bad guy. Or I wanted to.

Smokey Joe's, which we just call Smokes, is the most popular bar on campus. Everyone I know with a parent who went to Penn heard stories about Smokes when they were growing up. It's right in the middle of these seedy, random storefronts, a movie theater where someone was shot, and a tanning booth where Jane used to work until everyone told her she was way too tan. The sign on the door says "Smokey Joe's: The Pennstitution."

Inside there's a little entryway where you show your ID, and then you go either upstairs or downstairs. There are bars on both floors. On the lower floor there's dancing beside the row of scarred wooden booths. Upstairs, the bar is bigger. The floor is covered with little tables and there are booths along the side. I've been to Smokes hundreds of times, but I still don't know what it looks like exactly. We've never had dinner here or even seen it in daylight. And every time I've come I've been at least buzzed. In dreams I picture it only as a blur of people and glasses and plastic, checkered tablecloths.

Ryan seemed surprised at how everybody at Smokes knew me. But one of the bouncers had a crush on Susan and another one I had kissed, and Moe, the bartender, and I get along really well. Moe spotted me among the rest of the people in line and asked if I wanted my usual, so I said yes and also got Ryan a Rolling Rock. When Moe put the beer down in front of him, Ryan started to say something, but he paused a little, and Moe said, "Hold that thought," and went away to serve someone else.

Then Jared, Ryan's friend from that night at New Deck, showed up. It felt like a plant. When Ryan got up to go to the bathroom, Jared sidled up to me and whispered in my ear, "He was really psyched to impress you with how he knew the bartender here." I felt something close to giddiness just thinking that Ryan had wanted to impress me. He had to like me. Maybe his being a freshman was a good thing. He could be all mine. I'd have the chance to invent myself any way I wanted.

We left before closing. I couldn't wait to touch him. We went back to my high-rise and sat on the couch and watched *Cheers* reruns and fooled around and talked the rest of the night. His hands were so big. One hand could cover almost all of my ribs on one side. He made me feel small and almost protected, just as I'd imagined hundreds of times between the second he'd walked away before until that very moment.

When he kissed me, he used his hand to pull my face in, holding me as if I might go somewhere. I just couldn't let him go down my pants. Even though I wanted to, even though everything else felt so good. It just seemed like he would know so much then, like I had to

34

protect some things. I wasn't ready to trust him. He didn't push. We slept in our clothes on the floor in the living room. My roommates didn't even notice us there. He left before anyone woke up.

"I'll call you," he whispered as we stood in the doorway. The sky was a strange shade of indigo-purple. There was a shimmer around the buildings like a halo. He leaned down and kissed me. We kept not stopping. We had said so much that night. He had talked to me more about his parents and their divorce, and how hard it was on his mother, especially with the new girlfriend. He told me about helping his mother write her résumé. And I told him about my mother and the paper, how she made me feel so stupid, so without weight. I thought everything was out there. So I never seriously thought that he wouldn't call. But he never did. And Phoebe told me then that there was nothing that I could do.

I should be over Ryan, I think now. He was a freshman, and it was weeks ago, before the Sigma Chi party and the broken mirror, before the football game. But sitting on the bench in front of Steinberg-Deitrich now, alone, and without the helpfulness of a distraction, I realize how much I wanted Ryan to save me.

4
★
"driver 8"

I wipe my eyes with my sleeve and look down whenever people walk by. I'm trying to decide what to do next because I just really want to feel good again and I figure I'll go to the Palladium because by now it's late enough that the bars might be at least starting to fill up. And the Palladium is just across the Walk.

I haven't been to the Palladium in a while. The last time we went, we were just sneaking through the main room to the back door, which opened to the Gold Standard, a dance place below. We used this passageway out the back of the Palladium to avoid paying a cover or standing in line at the Gold Standard. There was a Theta party at the Gold Standard that night, and I had my hand on a thermos of Jacquin's vodka and grapefruit juice in the deep pocket of my party coat as I crept to the passageway while the Palladium bartender had his back turned.

Safely downstairs, I found Jane and we started dancing. She was seeing someone then, a rower named Sam, I think, who was very granola-sexy and rode a cool Trek bike everywhere, but she pointed out this guy to me who she thought was really hot. When I asked which one, she said, "Plaid shirt." So the rest of the night we referred to him as Plaid Shirt. He had dark, short hair and these intense green eyes with black, black lashes, and a few freckles. He looked kind of spacey, like he was stoned.

So finally, I got so drunk, I actually went up to him and said, "Dance with me, Plaid Shirt." And I had come to that point in the night, or that point in my drunkenness, I guess, where my dancing felt fluid, easy, and nicely blurred. I shook my hair out of its rubber band. We danced the whole time and then the lights came on without warning. We hadn't talked much. Afterward, we sailed out onto Locust Walk where I held hands with Plaid Shirt and Sam had his arm around Jane and they were walking home, his bike in tow. I told them to go ahead and then I followed Plaid Shirt into his fraternity house.

This was something I had vowed never to do, put myself in the hook-up position in someone's fraternity house. Because nothing's anonymous at this school, despite what you'd think from the size. A walk of shame the next morning would definitely make *34th Street*. And all kinds of weird shit happens at fraternity houses, like people watching you through secret holes in the wall. But there I was with basically a complete stranger. He had told me his name on the dance floor but straining to hear seemed like an unnecessary effort. And then I all of a sudden and without even any repartee or transition or anything, I was kissing Plaid Shirt. More like getting kissed by him.

He was not a good kisser, all teeth and angles. And I started to dehaze, which was extremely unappealing. So was sobering up to Plaid Shirt's messy room with boxers and airplane bottles of Jack everywhere. *I so do not want to be here,* I thought.

"I have to go," I said.

He grabbed my arm. His voice sounded blurred. "Why?" He seemed pathetic, whiny. Major buzz kill.

I rolled my eyes, ground my back teeth together, and swung my feet to the floor. "Umm, I need to get my keys and my ID back from Jane. She was holding them for me while I danced. They're still in her coat pocket." It could happen.

He sat up too, but held on to my arm so I couldn't stand. "Sweetheart, you don't need keys. Your roommates will let you in. Or you'll get an extra key from the desk. Whatever. Why worry? You're here now. Relax. We'll deal with it later, okay? You just gotta chill, girl. Stop stressing." He rubbed my shoulders in a way he must have imagined would soothe me. It made my stomach hurt.

"Uh, no, really, I think I should just go. " I pried his arm off and stood. "For now, you know. But I could come back or see you later or—"

He had followed me to the door. "Hey"—his voice had an edge now—"enough of that."

He positioned himself in the doorway with his arms pressed up on either side. I tried to pry one of his hands away, but this time he was ready; the muscles were tense and strong. "What's my name?" he asked. For a second, I pictured a phone ringing at my parents' house, someone calling to tell them something terrible had happened to their daughter. I pushed on his arm again and tried to slide out. "No," he said. "Do you seriously not know my name?"

I thought about screaming, but when I felt for my voice, it seemed like nothing was there. I wondered how things had turned so fast—from blurry and full of possibilities to razor-edged and scary.

"Man, what a heartbreaker you are." He shook his head, arms still up, locking me into this cage.

You fucking psycho. I willed my voice to come. When it did, it sounded low and soft and foreign. "Seriously, let's not make a bigger deal out of this than it needs to be. I kissed you. It was fun. Now I want to leave." My heart started to pound. *Why did I ever come here?*

Please, God, let me out of this room and I swear I'll stop doing this stupid shit—all this drinking, all this flirting, all this going places with guys I don't know. This—alone with strangers, nobody knowing where you are—is totally how women get raped.

Then finally he laughed this eerie, stoned laugh and said, "Fine, whatever, break my heart," and loosened his arm. I slid under it and maneuvered through the house and into the cool, pitch-black air.

But here I am, once again, back at the Palladium, looking for something.

I don't get nervous about walking into bars alone. I always think that eventually I'll see someone I know, anyway. I sit on a barstool and pick the sesame sticks and crunchy balls from a bowl of bar mix and order a vodka grapefruit. The place is pretty empty. The first sip of the drink is like the moment you realize your migraine is gone. It scares me a little, not necessarily because it's alcohol, but just to need anything so much, the instantness of the relief. I see my hand shake as I put down the glass. And then I wonder why I did because I pick it up again right away to go for more. I want that coldness and the comforting smell in my nostrils again—that smell feels like coming home. I sense the very beginnings of the numbness that will later snake down to my fingertips and toes. I twist my feet inside my cracked Stan Smiths.

I ask the bartender to watch my backpack while I go to the bathroom. I splash a little water on my face, look into the mirror, and get that wave of panic again, the vague sense of having forgotten something important, of not knowing the next step. I can hear R.E.M. singing but can't make out the song until I get into the hallway. It's "Driver 8," which makes my chest tighten. His singing is almost blurry: Does he say we can reach our destination or we can't?

Ryan Weiss is there, then, trying to get the bartender's attention with a twenty, his body making a long diagonal against the bar. I can see the pack of Camels outlined in the pocket of his flannel. I want to take a few steps back into the bathroom. To gather my thoughts. Think up some good one-liners. Possibly climb out the window. But I don't. And somehow I know my staying will change everything, even more than it's already changed since Number Six fumbled the ball.

The bartender isn't paying attention to Ryan, but he looks at me as I head back to the table and I jerk my head toward Ryan, like "Help out my friend here," which is nice, considering. If Ryan is shocked to see me or embarrassed that he never called, he doesn't let it show, just says, "Hey," like it's nothing that I'm here. So I slide back into my seat and sip my drink and listen to the Erasure song that's playing and wish I had musical talent, like then I'd be happy. Then I'd know what to do.

Of course, it's difficult to hear my own thoughts because my heart is basically thumping and roaring through my ears even though I know now what kind of a person he is. I can't help it. He sits down next to me and I bum a cigarette, waiting to hear how he'll craft his excuses this time, hoping he makes them good and believable, wanting the possibility of him back again in spite of myself.

"So," he starts, "I guess you're wondering why I never called."

"Guess I'm wondering a lot of things."

"The thing is I really like you. A lot. And I planned on calling you, and I was so glad that you called me that time, but, you know, I let a few days go by because I had this midterm, and then I felt like a total schmo, like you were sitting there thinking that I wasn't going to call, and then I couldn't somehow . . ."

And then it all becomes background noise, like the sound of television screen snow. I mean, it's sort of soothing how he's feeding me all this bullshit about how he likes me, because it's the bullshit I need to hear to make it okay in my head to go home with him. But beyond that I don't really care about its content and I already know that this guy will never be my soul mate. But it doesn't matter. It's okay just to be lied to well right now.

And to his credit, I mean, in the sense that he's not totally a liar, I really think he is a messed-up person, screwed up because of his parents' divorce, which was recent, and I can believe that's made him afraid or hesitant about relationships. Actually I'm the one who brings up sex, like let's just do it, because it just doesn't make sense not to anymore when I can't even remember all the reasons I had for waiting, and I just really want to be held, and I tell him the story about the fumbled ball, which he missed because he was in line at Abner's waiting for his cheese steak after he and his roommates got high. And I believe him when he tells me he understands. Tonight that's enough.

5
★
bumbling through

I wake up in the Quad in his metal twin bed, my skin and hair reeking of stale smoke. I've been sleeping with my hands pressed together under my cheek like a baby, and I pull my head up and then look at my hands, and in the bright light they seem so old, somehow, and for a few seconds I just watch the dust motes swirl around my fingers and wish I were still sleeping, still not knowing what it's like to wake up here with him.

I feel an emptiness that penetrates me totally, a sadness much deeper than before, like back in Steinberg-Deitrich with the paper triangle was the good old days, compared to this. That I just had sex for the first time is such a nothing—like songs are written about this? Remembering it makes me just want to get the hell out of here. He doesn't notice me as I peel the covers off and slide myself to the edge of the bed. I collect my clothes from the pile on the floor, pull on my jeans, button my oxford, tie my sneakers, fish around in my book bag for gum, and leave. He still doesn't move. I don't even have to shut the door quietly. He's sleeping so deeply, thrown across the bed, careless and unlined. I know he won't hear.

Everything hurts. I feel like I'm made of wood and hinges. Even my jeans are painful. I walk across the Quad averting my eyes from the beginnings of sun. The birds are chirping, but otherwise campus seems like a ghost town, McDonald's wrappers whipping against the brick walls and shards of amber beer glass shining on the slate paths, like smashed-out possibilities or promises. But as I pass through the tall, steel gates, I feel momentarily thrilled by the sensation of escape. I'm walking away unscathed, still me, after everything that's happened. I can go anywhere right now, maybe leave it all behind me. Only I don't know where to go.

So I go home. It's funny, I suddenly think, what I call home. The dorm room where I live. Something that switches year to year. My parents, the house where I grew up, just isn't my home. My old bedroom looks fake, like a dollhouse bedroom, like no one ever lived there, especially not a teenager. On the twin beds, my parents have put these scratchy bedcovers that they brought back from Greece. In between them, where my stereo used to be, is a new night table with a vase of dried flowers on it. They took down my bulletin board, where I used to hang all the Absolut ads and movie posters that they wouldn't let me hang on my walls. My mother keeps her out-of-season clothes in my closet. The last time I was there, I opened the door to hang up my clothes and it was crammed with winter coats. It doesn't fit, thinking that my parents even exist, here in this place where I do all these shots and show strangers parts of me my parents will never see. In my American Lit class, we read something by T. S. Eliot that said "home is where one starts from." I am starting from here.

I share the slow elevator with a girl from the floor below me who once tried to get me to join a Bible study group. I told her I'd vote for a wedge of cheese as long as it was pro choice, and that I thought Jesus was just a regular carpenter. She doesn't acknowledge me, just stares down at her feet for the entire ride. She's got a pink-and-white-checked laundry bag and wears pink, drugstore flip-flops. Her white tube socks bunch around the thong part. I hoist my backpack and stare at the red-lit numbers.

When I get to my floor, I notice that all the signs on the bulletin board have changed since I last looked. They announce a sundae night, an upcoming show by a female improv group, a French conversation club. I feel like I've never been here before, or maybe like I'm coming home from a war years later. In front of my door, I balance my backpack on one knee as I search for my keys. When I finally find them, I'm almost surprised they still fit.

Everyone is still asleep. I wash my face and put on a nightgown. My clock says 6:45 A.M. I pull back the covers and sink into my bed, trying to imagine that I've been home the whole time.

I can't sleep, though. I lie there wishing someone would wake up, even Maggie, who usually wakes up early to secure a carrel with good light in the stacks. But her door is closed, and I hear nothing. At seven-fifteen I give up, throw the covers back, and decide to go to Phoebe's. I turn the shower all the way to hot and stand there in the steam for a while. I open up a new bar of soap and wash everything twice. When I'm done, I take a fresh oxford out of my drawer and a baggy pair of chinos. I want my clothes to float around me, without actually touching. I hold them to my face knowing exactly how they'll smell, like baby powder and Bounce sheets. I inhale over and over.

Phoebe answers the door, rubbing her eyes. Looking at the stuff on Phoebe's dining room table—empty shot glasses, a vegetable steamer, a half-eaten bag of microwave popcorn—it crosses my mind that we never eat anything normal. We all couldn't wait to get off the meal plan so we could ply ourselves with fat-free everything and binge at Beijing in between. I can't remember the last time I sat down and had a traditional meal with three different parts—a vegetable, protein, and starch—everything warm.

"Hi," Phoebe says. "Are you okay? What happened to you last night? I saw Jane and Susan at Murph's and they had no idea where you were."

"I was at Ryan's. I want to tell you about it, but can we get out of here?"

"Wow. Sure. Where do you want to go?"

"Someplace with windows."

We go to the American Diner. It's cold outside, and I walk with my arms crossed in front of my chest. I order oatmeal. I spoon brown sugar onto the top and cradle the warm bowl with my hands. "Did Susan tell you about the game?" I ask.

"Yeah," Phoebe says, "but I kind of didn't understand what she was saying. Something about you having some sort of freak-out. I figured she didn't know what she was talking about."

"Do you ever think about what happens when a guy fumbles the ball? Does it ever make you sad or something?" There's a silence, and I watch Phoebe close her eyes a little and try to think. I find myself praying that she knows what I mean. Someone else needs to get this. I don't want to be out there alone.

"I know what you mean. I'm not sure if I've actually sat there feeling sad, or anything. The way they announce it, though, and say his name over the loudspeakers. It seems sort of humiliating."

"That's exactly it. And it just hit me, suddenly. I guess it's stupid. It's not like these football players go home and cry or something. But it was just how earlier, my mom had called me again. And she just gets so negative and the way she talks down to me. That tone of voice." I shiver and look at the ceiling for a minute. "I get off the phone and somehow she manages to make me feel—ashamed. She takes me from big to small with just thirty seconds of that voice, you know? She takes everything I think I'm doing that's good, or that I'm excited about, and somehow she makes it wrong or obvious. I guess the fumble thing just touched a nerve."

"I can totally see how that could happen."

"And you know how you do all these things, like going out every night, or even studying, so your days are all filled up and you don't really think about things, and then when you do, it all just seems so hard, when you're face-to-face with it like that? Remember freshman year, when you stayed with me for a few days because you had a mouse in your room? I never told you this, but when you left, I felt so lonely. Like I had no direction once you'd gone."

Phoebe nods her head and puts a hand on my forearm across the table.

"I've just suddenly started feeling like that all the time. I can't seem to shake it."

"Well, we'll do something tonight, something different. Get off campus. Maybe you need a change of scenery."

"Maybe," I say. "But is that just what you do, try to fill up the time?"

"What else is there to do? You were going to tell me about Ryan."

"I slept with him last night."

"What?" Phoebe signals for more coffee without taking her eyes off me. "Where did you even see him?"

"After the game. I went to the Palladium and he was there."

"Did he say anything about not calling?"

"Yeah, he had all these reasons. Like his parents' divorce made him all afraid of relationships, blah, blah, blah. It didn't matter. I just wanted to do it. I don't know why."

"You shouldn't feel bad about it. Everybody makes it this big deal. But it's just one more thing. I never understood why everyone acts like it's something so different from everything else. I hope you're not feeling like you shouldn't have done it."

"Not in the way of worrying about my reputation or something. He's a freshman. We don't even know any of the same people. But, you know, it was my first time. And it was just so uneventful. And even though I'm okay with it and I was the one who wanted to, I just don't like the feeling that somehow he's out there thinking he's pulling one over on me, like I'll just believe everything he says, like I'm so desperate."

"I'm sure he's not even deep enough to be thinking that," Phoebe says.

"Yeah, you're probably right. But that bothers me too, like it's just another cheese steak to him or something. And I feel like I wasted my first time."

"You know what, though? I did it the first time with my high school boyfriend. And we were totally serious and got this hotel room and had candles and music and everything. And he stole this wine from his brother. And that was so nothing either. You expect your life to be so transformed, but it just isn't. And believe me, looking back at that, I feel pretty stupid and embarrassed and everything else. I think you just do."

"But at least you knew he liked you back," I say. "I slept with Ryan after he never even called me. When I know he never will."

"Is that so different from my sleeping with Chevs? Were our feelings even real? I don't know. And, God, I slept with him plenty of times when he wasn't liking me back, it turns out. I just think that you can't think of it in such monumental terms. It's just movies and soap operas that make it all seem so softly lit and perfect and important. But it never is. We're not even twenty years old. We're just bumbling through. Having experiences."

6

★

styrofoam

"Want to go to the movies?" Phoebe asks after we pay the check.

"Sure. What is there to see?"

"Hamlet with Mel Gibson?"

"Okay. Let's walk there. I'm feeling not so good about my thighs."

We go back to our apartments to put on sneakers. By the time I get there, Susan's awake, going through the fridge.

"What are you doing?" she asks.

"Meeting Phoebe. Going to a movie."

"So are you all better?"

"I wasn't sick, Susan."

She closes the refrigerator door, turns, and looks at me. "What's that supposed to mean?"

"Nothing. I'm fine." I tie my sneakers and get up. "I gotta go. We might be doing something later too. Going somewhere off campus, maybe."

"Off campus?" Susan says. "But tonight's the Halloween party at Deke! You made that great costume."

I had forgotten all about it. I was going as Cliff's Notes. I'd gone to this dance store downtown for yellow tights and spent hours drawing stripes on them in black marker. "I just feel like getting away."

"But you love Deke parties! And we always go together."

"Yeah, I know. Just not tonight, okay?"

"Where did you go last night? I didn't even see you," Susan says.

"Nowhere."

"Well, whatever's going on with you, I don't see how going off campus is going to solve anything."

"Maybe it isn't," I say. "I gotta go. Phoebe's waiting outside." I leave Susan standing there holding her diet Coke.

Phoebe and I walk all the way to the Ritz theater downtown without checking movie times. It takes about forty-five minutes. The air and the walk feel good to me, like my body's becoming more attached to my brain. I realize that running used to do this for me, but I haven't been in weeks. "Do you mind that we're skipping Deke tonight?" I ask.

"Oh, yeah. No, I don't care; I had forgotten all about it," Phoebe says. "I don't even have a costume."

We're there in time for the first show and we stand around outside until it starts, eating Junior mints and smoking.

When the movie lets out we're starving. We walk down Chestnut Street to this Mexican place, order strawberry margaritas and salsa and chips and burritos. Some of the time we just sit and crunch without talking. That's okay, with Phoebe. I don't feel like every space needs filling.

"What do you feel like doing tonight?" Phoebe asks.

"Are the Spider Webs playing anywhere?" The Spider Webs are

this band that plays around Center City a lot. They have kind of a cult following on campus, but I've never heard them. Maybe it's about time.

Phoebe asks the bartender for a paper and we scan the Arts section. They're playing at Chaucers at eight. We've never been, but the address is in the paper. We kill time at the Mexican place for a few hours, drinking more margaritas and getting pretty buzzed. Then we hop a bus back to Center City. We stop into a Rite Aid and buy very black mascara, sparkly green eye shadow, and berry lip stain. We stand in the mirror section and do each other's makeup. Then Phoebe takes a comb from her back pocket, and we take turns flipping our heads upside down for volume. We get to Chaucers at seven. It's pretty empty. There are booths against the window, a jukebox, worn Oriental carpets everywhere, even on the ceiling, and spider plants. We sit at the bar. I order my usual.

I think how nice it is to be here. Like you really can get away. And the crowd looks different as they drift in. Older and less generic, without all the crew shirts and strategically worn baseball caps with bills that have been tied to bats with rubber bands so they fold just right. Then Phoebe taps my arm and gestures to a guy who's sat down alone beside me. He's good-looking, sandy blond and tan for this season, that lean, tennis-player body. Crinkly eyes. I catch myself assessing hook-up potential.

"You know who you look like?" he says when I look his way.

"No, who?" When I was little, strangers used to mistake me for the little girl from *The Goodbye Girl*. Since then, no one.

"Like Flea from the Red Hot Chili Peppers."

"Like Flea? He's a man!"

"I'm not saying you look like a man, though. And he's good-looking."

Phoebe rolls her eyes. "You are not even talking about Flea, stupid," she says. "You mean Anthony Kiedis, the lead singer."

"Thanks a lot, Phoebe! So you think I look like him too?"

"No, not at all," Phoebe says. "Just the hair."

"My hair looks like a man's?"

"His hair looks like a woman's," the guy says. "He's got that nice, straight, long hair. I'm Trey."

"Trés what?"

"Ha ha. Trey as in I'm a third." At least he seems embarrassed about this.

"Oh." I shake his hand and hold on a little too long. "Rebecca. Beck. And that's Phoebe."

"Nice mole," he says, meaning this flat, brown dot near my eye.

"Have you not insulted me enough this evening?"

"No, I mean it. It's . . . I like it."

I stare into my drink. "Thanks. So, you look—older."

"So now you're going to insult me back?"

"No, I just meant . . ."

"Are you an undergrad?" he asks.

"Yeah. Sophomore."

"I'm in my first year at Wharton grad. Is that a problem?"

So he's already suggesting that something's going to happen. I wonder if I'm supposed to stop things, if normal people do, from automatically sliding into something more so easily. It's always this way, at a bar, buzzed, a guy comes into the picture; it's always something more beginning. I try to think back to a single time when it wasn't. Maybe with someone else's boyfriend, but that's all. Something must be wrong with me, that my stop mechanism is never working, but it's so hard, when you're blurred and unsharp, to crisp things up, to slow the downhill, to do anything other, really. My head hurts. Phoebe kicks me under the table and smiles.

"No. It's not a problem." I vacuum up the last sips of my drink and order another. The band arrives, just two women. They unpack guitars and set up the rest of their equipment. The waitress brings them big glasses of water. I like their calming hippie look—wide-leg pants, long hair. Then they begin to play, starting with the 10,000 Maniacs song about child abuse. The lead singer sounds just like Natalie Merchant. This is mostly what they play, covers of songs sung by women—k. d. lang, Sinéad O'Connor, lots of Indigo Girls—some original stuff, which is also good. It affects me, the way they lean so purposefully forward into their microphones and hold them in both hands. I wish that I could feel so deeply about something. I wish that I could get that far away. They close their eyes and sway.

Trey, Phoebe, and I don't talk while they perform, just signal the bartender for more drinks. Trey and I are so close our shoulders touch, so I have to move away just a little to see if he'll make them touch again, to see if it's on purpose. He does.

By the time the Spider Webs do their encore, I notice my words are a little muddled when I ask for another drink. They sing "Closer to Fine" and everyone gets up to dance in the tiny space. I remember standing at the tamale truck outside of Deke at the end of freshman year and watching the sun come up when Maggie started shouting the same song at the top of her lungs and I joined in: "I spent four years prostrate to the higher mind, got my paper and I was free!" That song made us feel so rebellious, skipping around West Philly in the middle of the night, but it didn't quite fit, now that I think about it. We felt free already and feared that after freshman year we'd feel less like that.

"Going to the Pub, Trey?" the waitress asks.

She's pretty, freckled, and athletic-looking, that cute, tan, small-nosed country-club type.

"Kate, this is Beck. And Phoebe," he says, gesturing to each of us in turn. He looks at his watch and then at me.

"Nice to meet you." I look down at my drink again. Kate walks away without getting an answer about the Pub.

"The Pub is this other bar on the corner. It's open later. We all

58

usually go there after. Do you want to come along?" Trey asks us.

"Beck, if it's okay with you, I think I'm going to head back. I'm pretty exhausted," Phoebe says.

"Are you sure? I was thinking I might go," I say.

"Yeah. But you should go. I'll catch a taxi."

"Okay," I say.

"Walk me out." Phoebe has a real taxi whistle. We hug good-bye while the driver waits.

"Are you sure you're all right?" Phoebe asks.

"Yeah. I'm fine."

"Be careful. Call me if you need me."

I'm happy that she doesn't give me the lecture about how fooling around with another guy isn't going to make me feel any better or less empty or take away any of whatever the Ryan thing has done to me. I already know. I make my way back to the bar and Trey.

We finish our drinks and he pays. Then it's time to go to the Pub. He has to put his arm around my back to steady me as I slide off the stool. I thank the Spider Webs as they pack up their things. We part the crowds that slowly make their various ways into the moonlight. The cobblestones under my feet look like waves. I touch my cold cheeks with the pads of my fingers.

I peek inside the door to the Pub while we wait in line to be carded. This is a place I know I couldn't handle sober. It's so crowded, you can't move without touching someone. I flash my ID (a gift from a Swedish exchange student; I'm twenty-eight) and I'm in, smothered on all sides by Polo oxfords like billowed sails.

It's hot. I'm glad I put my camisole on. I take my oxford off and tie it around my waist. Something in the air feels vaguely like a fight waiting to happen. No one here looks old enough to be twenty-one. Everyone screams to be heard. Fluorescent-painted drink specials line the walls offering cheap pitchers and shots of Jägermeister. I'm sure there's no toilet paper. People check each other out in that merciless or maybe sad way people check each other out late night. I wonder if it was a mistake to come.

Everyone's smoking cigarettes and drinking bottled beers or pink drinks in plastic cups. For a moment I think I've lost Trey, but then I see his braceleted hand stretched out in front of me. We push toward the bar where I order a vodka shot and a vodka grapefruit. The first taste makes me know I can handle this scene. I probably don't need the shot, but I have it anyway. Trey laughs at how I down it before he can even take his money out. He orders me another.

My drinking skill makes me kind of a novelty with guys. Nate Rosen loves to show me off like a magic act. At Sigma Chi formals I went to when I was dating Scott Childs last year, Nate would elbow some of his brothers. "Check this out," he'd say, pointing to me as I nervously juggled three shots and a chaser, each in its own plastic cup. I'd protest, but he'd always insist. "Check this out. This kid's like one-oh-five soaking wet too." Then I'd turn my body to the bar for a little privacy and down it all. "You're the best, kid," Nate would say each time I'd finished. Sometimes I like that he calls me kid. I imagine that's how it is to have an older brother. Sometimes I have a crush on him and I don't want him to call me kid anymore.

Trey and I find the only corner where we can stand. I'm up against the wall. He leans toward me and braces himself with one arm. He stands so close I can smell his breath like Doublemint gum and tobacco. He leans in even closer so I can't do anything but breathe him. He talks to me about his senior year at Cornell, lightweight football, dissatisfaction, this story about a hitchhiker. I want to see the tattoo that everyone on his football team got. He unzips his pants and pushes down his boxers to show me. It's a red football helmet, right above his pelvic bone. I run my finger over it. Then he buckles up and tucks the tails of his shirt back in. I feel a bit shaky on ıy feet. I rest my palm at the base of his stomach to steady myself.

When I was little, my mother could never make it to day care efore closing, so I'd go home with the day care woman. At her ouse, her daughter would always bring out this rock collection. She ad amethysts, geodes, and fool's gold, but I'd always pick out this ny pouch filled with plain-colored stones that had been polished so mooth and shiny, my hands yearned for them. When I left, I'd always sk to take them with me. Touching Trey is like that. His body is so mooth; once I touch him, I just want to touch him again, and I keep oing back, punctuating every sentence by reaching for him.

"So the waitress, Kate," he says. "I've known her for years." I /onder why he's explaining this to me. Has he hooked up with her? ; he trying to tell me they're together? I strain to look relaxed.

"I grew up here. My parents live up on Delancey. Her parents new mine from summers, the Shore. We both stayed at LBI, like two ouses away on the beach. She got expelled from Dana Hall, down ı Boston, for drinking in the music room or something. That was her econd boarding school. Her parents kicked her out, did this tough-)ve thing. She's been on her own ever since. She lives in Manneunk ow. She hasn't even heard from them in over a year."

"That's terrible." I think about my own fight with my mother efore the game, how much worse off Kate is than me. "Are you"—I ıel so stupid asking—"are you together?"

"God, no. Everyone thinks so, though. More like brother and ister. I shouldn't tell you this, but, her boyfriend hits her." I must look oubtful because Trey says, "No, really, one time she came to me rying because he had bitten her, can you believe that? Grabbed her nd bit her cheek until it bled. I called this lawyer friend of my dad's, nd we were all set to press charges. At the last minute she backed own, said she'd made up." He shakes his head and takes a long pull n his Jack Daniel's.

61

I look for Kate across the bar but can't pick her out among all the others, girls in jeans with Laura Ashley patches and hair streaked a lemony color in front, girls, I think suddenly, who maybe have their own secrets.

That's the last thing I remember, looking around the Pub for Kate, wanting to see her. The next thing I know, it's morning. When I first open my eyes, I think I'm back in Baltimore in my twin bed in my old room. I look around. I have no idea where I am. I flop back on the bed. "Stay calm, stay calm," I whisper. "You're okay."

I think of last year at Halloween when we went party hopping, and I'd dressed as night, just an excuse to wear a tight, new black Benetton knit dress. I cut stars out of poster paper and pinned them all over me. I woke up on the back stairs of the Quad the day after. Some agonizing rays of light poking through the wrought iron window jarred me from this dream I was having where I had an extremely bad headache and my ears were ringing with this sound like dog whistles. I was wearing my dress but no longer had any of the stars. Then I saw some scattered on the floor. So I followed this white-star trail down the steps and across to the front gate of the Quad. I must have begun taking them off as I walked into the Quad, to get a head start on undressing. Then I'd just petered out and flopped onto the stairwell.

The sheets are cool, crisp, and tightly tucked. I see another twin bed beside me with a lump in it, but have no idea who's in there. There's a bucket next to me. Somebody must have thought I would puke. There's a big color TV with a remote control and a brick fireplace and a bay window with cushions in it and poufed, pastel curtains like wedding cake icing. The curtains aren't totally drawn; I blink against the sun. My head throbs.

I'm wearing underwear and the camisole I had on the night before. My hair smells like stale smoke. Oh, my God. Trey. This must be Trey's parents' house. And they're out of town. But I don't think it's

Trey in the bed beside mine. I can't remember if anything happened with him. I look at the clock on the window ledge. Noon. Fortunately, I don't return my parents' phone calls a lot of the time anyway, so they shouldn't think it's anything unusual. The lump moves and I recognize the waitress, Kate, the one Trey had talked about.

"Hi," she says groggily, pushing her hair out of her face.

She's got a black eye. I will my face not to register a reaction. "Hi. I know you're Kate . . . but I don't remember . . ."

"You know this is Trey's?"

I nod.

"You were pretty wasted last night. We were impressed, though. You didn't boot."

Thank God. "How did we end up here?" I ask.

"Trey brought us both back because Rich and I got in a fight. My boyfriend."

I start to remember. "Oh, I'm so sorry that happened. Are you—"

"Is it bad?" She points to her eye.

"It's not good."

"Anyway, Trey called the cops on him and it was this big scene at the Pub. Trey had to wait for them to show up and answer questions. They let me go home and clean up and stuff so he gave us the keys to his place. Trey didn't think I was safe at my own apartment. He wants to save the world, you know?"

I nod. I don't, though. I don't know anything about Trey. I feel like I should be somewhere alone, that I should take a time-out somehow and think about why I'm here. Trey, Ryan, Plaid Shirt, what I'm doing. I feel like I never get time to actually think. I never seem to process anything. And I'm never alone.

"I helped you undress, in case you were wondering. I just thought you'd be more comfortable."

I exhale. "Thanks. Trey's not here?"

63

"His room's at the other end of the hall, but I think he went out to get breakfast stuff. I'm starving. Aren't you?"

"Why did he hit you?" I ask, then think it sounds too harsh. Presumptuous too. I hardly know her. "I'm sorry."

"No, it's okay. I know everyone wants to ask it. Rich always thinks there's something going on between me and Trey. It's especially bad when he's drinking. He's not a bad person. He just gets so possessive."

I don't know what to say because I can't imagine letting some guy hit me. But then I think about Ryan and how I let him suck me in just because I felt alone, and about Plaid Shirt and that moment when he stood in the doorway and wouldn't let me leave. It's not so different.

I don't want to say I understand what she's going through, because I probably don't. So instead I tell her about Ryan, including how I slept with him, and even a little bit about the fumbled ball at the football game, and why it made me so sad. I can tell by the way she looks at me that I'm making her feel better, though she doesn't say much, just nods and keeps pushing her hair behind her ears.

Then Trey walks in with a white paper bag of bagels, a carton of OJ, and a stack of glasses. "Good morning, sunshines," he says, and we all devour everything without much conversation and scrounge around for cigarettes. Then Kate runs out to the corner for coffees since Trey doesn't know how to work his parents' machine.

Trey sits down on the bed next to me. I want to really look at him. I want to face this, to remember what the point of the whole thing was. I keep going back to the feel of his stomach under my palm from the night before. I worry about what's going to happen now that we're alone. I don't know what I want to happen. He's wearing flat-front chinos that hang down low. His shirt's buttoned only in the center.

"How are you doing?" he asks.

I shrug and smooth the sheets around me to make sure nothing's showing. I rub my head, pushing on my temples with my fingers. "What are you scared of?" he asks softly.

Everything. What am I not scared of? Morning. This. My lack of a plan. I don't answer. Then he reaches out and I suck in my breath as he holds my face in his hand and looks at me. He pushes the hair out of my eyes. I know he's going to kiss me, but I move away just enough and reach for my pants beside the bed and start sliding them on under the covers, buying time. I wish I didn't want to kiss him back. Not like I think Trey is like Rich or all guys are, just that I want to be the kind of person who can stand alone. I remember finding this journal that our second-grade teacher had made us keep and my first page said: "I want to have some iventures." So I started independent and then became dependent, like growing shorter.

"I am so attracted to you, Rebecca." He moves my face back, makes me look at him again.

It's exactly the right thing to say, of course, especially to me, since I always think my looks are more the kind that grow on you. At the same time it's almost obligatory to tell me this after we've spent so much charged time together, and fooling around now seems almost obligatory too, almost like we've already done it except that we haven't because of the strange, fluky circumstances. I could just sleep with him now and still be okay, but I already know the hollowed-out way I'll feel afterward, like a styrofoam cup. I kiss back anyway. And then he's touching me all over and everything is good and not good both. I'm rolling down a buttery hill again. Fast and out of control.

"Kate will be back soon," I say.

"You're right." He pulls his hand from inside my chinos. "Are you okay?"

I exhale shakily, relieved, and wonder briefly how I would have stopped things if I didn't have this excuse. At least I've stopped things. This time. "I just need to protect myself right now," I say.

"I know."

I wonder how he knows. Is it just that he can read me, because he's older? Or is it something I said the night before? I can't remember what we talked about. This is a blackout. I had a blackout. I remember laughing at the AA guy who came to lecture us in high school, when he talked about missing whole days and nights. How we thought he was such a loser.

Trey leaves the room and comes back with a stack of fluffy yellow towels. "Here you go. For your shower. Second door on the left." Then he walks away.

I take a long, hot shower in his white-tiled bathroom, looking up at the pure blue through the skylight. The steam fills the bathroom and smells faintly vodkalike. I wrap my body and my head in towels and walk back into the guest room. Kate's there now, and she and Trey are sitting on the floor drinking coffee. Kate hands me a cup. I sit down on the floor with them. The coffee tastes sweet and milky, just the way I like it. It helps my head. This seems like a better way to end things. Kate lights a cigarette and Trey takes one out of his pocket, lights it off Kate's, and hands it to me. "None for you?" I ask, relaxing into the first drag.

"Nope. My turn to shower." He rises and stands in the doorway. "Will you be here when I'm done?"

"I don't think so."

"Then c'mere."

I go to him. He hugs me and kisses my cheek. "Maybe I'll see you again?" he asks.

"Maybe." *I don't know what I'm doing. I have no plan.* "Bye. I had fun." Kate and I sit back down on the floor and finish our cigarettes. I'm starting to get that cabin-fevery feeling like on a Sunday after a good weekend and you don't know what to do. I want to be outside.

I look at my watch. "Wow, I really have to get back to school." It's Monday. I've already missed Art History. I'm taking twentieth-century art this semester.

"I wish I was in school sometimes. You're lucky," Kate says, crushing her cigarette into the ashtray beside her even after it's already out.

This is something my parents usually say. But it's different, coming from Kate. I *am* lucky. At this good school, all paid for, no job, nothing to do but schoolwork. All the time in the world to fall apart. Sick lucky. I'd be an asshole to look her in the eye and not admit it. Yeah, I know."

Kate has draped my sweater from last night on the chair by the window and opened it a little to air out the smoke. "Thank you," I say, putting it on. Kate and I hug good-bye too. I leave this small book of poetry I usually carry around by Judith Steinberg on the bedside table for her when her back is turned. There's this poem called "Lillian's Lament," where the narrator tries to make herself what this man wants; she burns off her hair and wears a blond wig, cuts off her arms so as not to be clinging, and in the end when she's left with nothing, not even her tongue to express herself, then he says, So close, so close.

7

float like butterfly

I walk back home the way Phoebe and I came when we went to the movie, shivering. I squint in the light, remembering how my mother told me always to carry sunglasses because squinting makes permanent wrinkles.

I feel sad that I've missed Art History. There are probably 150 of us in a giant lecture hall, and it's not like anyone will notice. In fact, the Monday class always seems to have more holes than students. But I like this professor, not the TA, but the actual professor; she's so lively and interesting. And the course doesn't fulfill a credit for me; I have all my credits in the Arts and Letters column already, but I chose it as an elective anyway, specifically to learn about modern art, which I really love. It seems somehow like exactly the kind of subject you're supposed to learn about in college.

I always sit in the same seat, up close, with this random Phi Delt named Duncan MacAllister. It's so funny to me how we seek each other out, even though we aren't friends, only friends of friends', part of the same general circle. He always saves me a seat

and we both scribble notes furiously, stopping only to laugh at someone who's snoring or asking a stupid question. I've developed a routine. I come to class in "disguise." I wake up, chug a diet Coke, put on
the first thing I can grab, wrap my head in a scarf, don my Ray•Bans,
and smear on some bright red lipstick. I take Spruce Street, of
course, never the Walk. The goal is to make it to class and back without being recognized, except by Duncan MacAllister, who thinks it's
the funniest thing he's ever seen. I barely make it through class, sip-
ping an extra large coffee and munching on Tylenols and a greasy
egg sandwich or a buttered chocolate-chip muffin from the breakfast
truck. Then I scurry back home, shut all my shades, and flop back
into bed until it's time to get ready to go out that night. Today is the
only time I've skipped this ritual. I wonder if Duncan will be worried.

I decide to stop at the Art Museum on the way home; maybe
it's because I want to feel better somehow for missing class. We've
been there a few times in our discussion groups, but only to look at
specific things. This is the first time I've been alone, the first time I've
been to any museum alone. I feel a tension, almost a knot of antici-
pation, as I walk up the steps where Rocky runs in the movie.

When we come for class, we have to talk or listen, either share
our thoughts or explain our opinions or hear the TA spout all of her
latest theories. I don't know, sometimes when she goes off like that,
about "an ode to shrugging off the constraints of the linear" or whatever, I feel like saying, "The emperor has no clothes!" After a certain
point, it just seems so phony. We never just say how it makes you feel
or talk about anything real, like compare it to a song or a situation
that might really mean something.

When I go to museums with my parents, they never just let me
look at the modern stuff, even though they like modern art too. "You
have to know what came before," they say, "to have any opinion of
what comes after. You have to explore the whys." I guess they have a

point. And that's why I'm taking Art History. But it's a class, and that's how I want to learn the whys, not on some random weekend when I just want to look at Jasper Johns flags. With my parents, you have to explore the whys every single time, even on weekends.

So today, as I start to run up the Rocky steps, my heart is really beating, because it's mine today, and I can just look at the modern stuff, fuck the stupid impressionism and lilies and those choppy bronze sculptures of women or goats or whatever; I never understand what their purpose is. Like seeing this image of a goat, what is that supposed to do for me? It's just a goat. Today I can start where I want to start.

The first painting I see when I walk through the gateway into the modern wing is new since the last time I was here with my recitation. It's a six-foot, whitish canvas with words that look as if they were made with those plastic stencils so there are these cuts of light between parts of the black-painted letters, like where the two parts of *L* would meet. And even though it's stencils, it's not perfect. There are these little excess drips of paint. And the letters spell out FLOAT LIKE BUTTERFLY STING LIKE BEE.

The artist took out the articles, so it's not "float like uh butterfly sting like uh bee" when you read it to yourself. It's as if that painter knew that the words were powerful enough to stand alone. Like words that are so tough, a chant you can repeat over and over, shouldn't be held back by dumb little language rules. We want to think of those words as busting out of the rules, off the canvas, charged. Float Like Butterfly. Sting Like Bee.

I take a few steps back and look again. When I think about it some more, it's sad, in a way too, because those power words were about Muhammad Ali, who has Parkinson's disease. And didn't he get so bashed up from all the fights that in the end he lost his strength?

72

And it's there again: that feeling of sorrow mixed with nothingness. There's something hard to think about—maybe it's about Kate or Ryan or losing my virginity; or missing class; or my mom, and that tone of voice that cut me into nothingness the morning of the game, telling me my ideas had no worth; or Muhammad Ali having Parkinson's disease; or Number Six fumbling the ball. That was me out there, alone in front of all those people, dropping the ball, failing. I feel it physically, my stomach tightening, achy. And I look around the museum and everyone seems so purposeful, tour groups propelled through life by their fanny packs and the words coming through their headphones, describing these paintings so neatly, so easily. All the loose ends wrapped up.

I can remember a few times before where I've felt alone in a room full of people, times when I was drunk and could barely concentrate on a conversation, my own little universe of thoughts pounding around. Or looking up from an exam and seeing everyone around me frantically scribbling, thinking for one, horrified second, I'm finally going to screw up. But I've always snapped out of it, concentrated on the beat of some great New Order song and the movements of my feet on the beer-smeared floor, put my head down and cranked out another four-blue-book analysis of rose-colored stained-glass and cloak images in Yeats's poetry. But this time it's different, and I'm starting to know it. No cup of coffee or cigarette or drink or fooling around seems a good enough diversion.

8
★
give me a smile

I'm back out on Walnut Street, sucking in the bracing air like I'm eating, like it's tangible, panting, and rummaging in my backpack for cigarettes. I'm getting hungry, so I go to the food court and order crisscut fries. It's early, but some people are here having lunch between classes, so I sit in the farthest corner table I can find. People share the connected tables here, so I keep sort of peeking out to the side while I read a magazine someone's left behind, and reaching for my fries from the folded red-and-white paper container on the table beside me.

Then this guy sits down diagonally across from me who looks kind of bum-ish, I guess you could say, but like a bum who cares, safety pins placed carefully, symmetrically, all the way down each coat sleeve. I've seen him before, in the library reading the newspaper. And I kind of feel grossed out by him, which I know is really shitty, so I try not to. But then he reaches over, I swear to God, and takes one of my fries. Right out of my container.

Okay, I admit it, I'm trying to restrain myself from picking up my fries and moving. But I figure I'll just take one and he'll see that they are *my fries* and not touch them, maybe even slink away. So I make this big deal about fishing out this long fry, putting ketchup on it. Then I go back to my magazine, crunching as loudly as possible. But he does it again, sort of quietly pulls out a fry from my pile and eats it.

I look up to see if anyone else is watching this. No one seems to be. I clear my throat, kind of glare at the guy, and eat another one. This goes on until all the fries are gone: he takes one, I take one. I'm so appalled by this man, and I think about how gross it is that I'm sharing my fries with him. And then he gets up, throws his napkins into the trash can, and leaves. I fold up my magazine and kind of shake my head. It's not like I can afford all the fries in the world right now, either; I've been rationing carefully this month. Then I see them: my own fries, untouched, on the other side of the counter beside me.

I leave, rattled. I'm walking back toward campus, deciding what I'm going to do next and wishing I had some plans laid out for me, or not; I'm not sure. Maybe I should take some time and sit somewhere and think about things, but it just seems so daunting and lonely. And I'm wondering about why I'm basically inhuman, assuming that the man was stealing from me, when I was actually stealing from him and he was the gracious one, letting me, and maybe not knowing where his next fries would come from, when this guy on the street says, "Got a cigarette, baby?"

I'm still really thinking hard about the fries so I barely hear, but I do hear him when I get a little closer and he says, "Oh, come on, give me a smile."

And I'm pissed because I don't need to be instructed to get happy by a total stranger. Why does everyone feel like it's okay to tell me how to be? Susan wanting me to cheer up, and my mother telling me I'm not scholarly enough. I'm so sick of letting people just traipse right through my life with their expectations and demands and not having the guts to say *stop*.

That's when something clicks in me.

Looking back on it, I suppose that this could have been dangerous. But this man just assumes I could be thinking nothing of importance as I walk down these streets, contemplating the guy in the food court, the fries, my character flaws, the inhumanity of people to other people. As if he's entitled not only to step right in, but actually tell me how I should feel, tell me how to remodel myself to please him. So I walk by and ignore the guy, but then I actually stop on the sidewalk and step back to where he's sitting. And every part of me clenches. *Float like butterfly. Sting like bee.*

I stare into his eyes. He must be shocked that I don't just keep going, because he doesn't move at all. I make my jaw really firm and I say really slowly, "Look. I am *not* your baby and I do *not* have to smile for you." Then I walk away fast, because I know what his next word probably is.

I veer up Locust Walk, smiling hard. I exhale and just say *"Yes!"* right out loud.

Back at home everyone is just waking up, except Maggie, who's already at the library. Jane and Susan are sitting around in boxers and T-shirts talking about the Halloween party. Jane was a big hit; she and another girl in her sorority both went as gum under a sneaker—pink fuzzy sweater, pink tube skirt, sneaker tied to a pink baseball hat—and she hooked up with this Deke guy again. He had just left. He asked her to go to his formal tonight, so she has to throw together some kind of outfit.

"Where have you been?" asks Susan, like she's mad at me.

"Out with Phoebe."

"Out where? We never saw you."

"Off campus. We went to hear a band."

Jane and Susan exchange a look. "But you never came home!" Jane squeaks. I picture dogs all over West Philadelphia pricking up their ears. "Were you with the freshman?"

"No, Jane. I was not with the freshman."

"What's going on with him, anyway?" Susan says.

"Nothing."

"Well, that's good."

"Why is that good?" I ask.

"Because," Susan says, "you could do so much better."

"You don't even know him," I say. I guess she's right, but for all of the wrong reasons. Or maybe she's wrong; maybe there is something really great in Ryan; maybe I just haven't found it, haven't done the right things to crack the code.

"But he's a freshman. And now is, like, the time of our lives. We're in our prime. You can date whoever you want. You don't have to lower yourself to waiting around for some freshman who lied to you," Jane says, fishing her hand in a bowl of popcorn and then crunching on a bunch of unpopped kernels.

"Thanks for the support," I say.

"What was wrong with Scott Childs?" asks Susan. "He asked about you at the party last night."

I've dated Scott Childs on and off. He's good in a way my mother would like, in a way Susan can understand: a junior, dual-degreeing with Wharton, Sigma Chi, but not the typical Sigma Chi—not Grosse Pointe, lacrosse or squash player, blond, lighthearted. He's from Maine, and he has this weightiness to him, like there's always something on his mind. And maybe he's good for me; I don't know. He's the kind of guy where you don't sit there and worry if he can get the waiter's attention. Once I took the train to New York just to buy a pink dress for his formal because he said everyone wore black too much. He came to my door with a dozen roses, looked around at my roommates, and said, "Hey, girls." And he looked at me and the pink dress like he was genuinely appreciative.

The thing is, I was never sure how I felt about Scott when we were together, and it scared me sometimes that he seemed pretty into the relationship. He'd get drunk at parties and embarrass me when I'd dance with one of his fraternity brothers. He'd confess this undying love for me in blurred answering-machine messages with loud music in the background that scared me in the morning. Even though ostensibly I wanted a boyfriend, when these boyfriendlike things would start to happen, it somehow made me feel as if my options were being closed off and something too permanent was starting. I guess I believe in fate or some higher power, but I don't believe in my own ability to listen to it, so I'm always wondering if the choices I make are somehow interfering with the course that's intended for me and changing my life forever and for the worse. That's why I ended things with Scott Childs.

"Nothing's wrong with Scott Childs," I say. "Why don't you go out with him? And I was with a grad student last night, if that's old enough for you."

"Trey?" Jane says, giggling.

"How did you know?"

"He called. Here." She hands me a message. I am not as excited as I should be. But if I call him, I'll have a plan. I call Trey.

"Hey," he says.

"Hey. How did you get my number?"

"It was on the book you left for Kate. That was a cool thing to do, by the way."

"It was stupid. I feel like I want to help her but there's nothing I can do."

"She really liked it. It meant something to her."

"I don't know," I say. "I'm just this stupid sophomore. I don't have a clue about her problems."

"That doesn't make you a bad person, you know. Just wanting to understand is pretty good."

But I don't think so.

"So," Trey says, "did you really never want to see me again?"

"I don't know." I really don't.

He laughs. "Well, if I can pull you away from the frat scene one more night, I'd like to take you out."

I hate that I'm so readable, that he knows without knowing me that I'm into the "frat scene." "Okay," I say.

"Whoa, calm down. You sound a little too excited."

"I'm sorry, Trey. I don't mean to sound unexcited. I've just been kind of sad lately."

"I know, you told me. The fumbled football, and that thing with your mom."

I still don't remember telling him. When he says it back to me now, it seems so dumb. It doesn't make any sense.

"Where do you want to go?" he says.

But I've never been any places off campus except the places we went the night before. Then I remember Backstreets, the bar Ryan said he liked. It was sort of on campus, sort of not. "How about Backstreets?"

Trey laughs. "Interesting choice. But you're an interesting girl. Sounds good. I'll pick you up."

"At my dorm?"

"Yes, at your dorm. I do realize that you're a sophomore and live in a dorm. Do you want to go to dinner first?"

"No thanks. I have dinner plans with my roommates." I can't picture myself sitting through a whole dinner with Trey. I give him directions and tell him to meet me downstairs. I don't want to deal with the whole process of signing him in at the desk and the roommate inspection.

"Well, that's interesting," says Susan when I hang up.

"Not really," I say, wondering what I'm going to do until nine, when Trey gets here.

I'm out of cigarettes and I don't want to leave the house, so I get everyone to order from Pete's Pizza. They deliver, including cigarettes. We all order diet Cokes and ravioli and eat it out of the aluminum containers. Jane just picks at hers, of course, moving it from side to side with her fork, and then she steams a whole head of broccoli and eats it with her hands, tearing it into individual trees. Afterward, I sit in the window and smoke while we work on getting Jane ready for the formal.

"Why do you think he asked me so last minute?" she wants to know. "Should I be insulted? Should I say anything?"

Guys around here do that all the time. They wait until the night before and then get drunk enough to get their courage up. Most of the fraternities have cocktail parties the night before their formals just to get a pool of potential last-minute dates. Scott Childs told me that the big joke is whether you'll recognize which one's your date when you go to pick her up and whether she'll turn out the way you expected or whether she'll turn out to be, as Scott put it, "a real bow wow."

"Maybe he's shy," Susan says. "Definitely do not say anything."

Jane moans and makes her sad face.

I don't want to loan Jane a dress because the last one she borrowed ended up torn when she fell in the beer gouge while she was dancing in the basement. Plus she walked around for days telling everyone how tea length on me was full length for her and giggling. I just can't handle all that "Oh, I'm so tiny and adorable" BS.

Fortunately she finds something in Susan's closet. It's too froufrou for me, lavender taffeta with a cluster of flowers at the back.

"You're acting weird, Beck," Susan says as we're trying different rhinestone necklaces. "What's up?" But the phone rings before I have to answer her. It's Phoebe.

"What happened last night?" Phoebe asks.

I drag the phone into my room and shut the door. "Nothing. I just passed out at his place. We barely even fooled around."

"You were really drinking."

"I know."

She doesn't push me. "He's really cute."

"You think so?"

"Oh, yeah. And wouldn't it be great to date someone who doesn't even go here?"

"I guess." I wonder if I am less excited than I should be about this just because nothing is wrong. Trey's a good guy. Smart. He seems to like me. There's just no danger. "We're going out tonight."

"Are you serious?"

"Yeah. Do you want to come over? We're getting Jane ready for the Deke formal."

"Maybe after she leaves." Phoebe doesn't really like Jane and Susan, but they never seem to notice. They still like Phoebe.

"Okay. She's leaving at seven-thirty. And Susan has a Tabard meeting at seven."

"I'll be there at eight."

At seven, I put on a going-out mix tape with all these Go-Go's songs on it and pour Jane a drink to calm her nerves. Her date is a half an hour late; he arrives with Phoebe. He looks wasted. He has three red roses. Jane hands them to me in the paper cone without moving her eyes off him. "Take care of these for me," she says.

"Sure, no problem. Have fun tonight, you guys."

She leaves without a coat or a good-bye, giggling.

Phoebe and I sit down at the table, and she picks at my leftover ravioli. "So tell me more about last night," she says. "Are you feeling any better?"

"Not really. Pretty much the same. Can I ask you a question?"

"Sure, what's up?"

"Do you know anyone whose boyfriend hits them?" I ask.

"I don't think so, why?"

"You know the waitress at Chaucers, you met her, Trey's friend Kate. Her boyfriend hits her. I was just wondering about it."

"Well, think about all the things that go on around here. Did you read that Peggy Sanday book?"

Fraternity Gang Rape? Parts of it."

"So you know what it's about," Phoebe says. "What fraternities do during hell week, how the bonding rituals are so dehumanizing and teach the brothers to equate women with weakness, and about all of these rapes, and other rapelike things that go on. I think it's kind of the same, not exactly the same, but coming from the same place."

"That's kind of what I was thinking," I say.

"We've all thought it, I think, to some degree. It's like, why do women just like us let all that stuff happen? It has to be because of some kind of bigger thing, some kind of societal thing, that tells us that it's okay, somehow. There's this part in the book about 'beaching,' where this fraternity with a deck around the second floor tells the brothers who are hooking up there at night to flash the lights inside, and then the rest of the brothers go up on the deck and sit there in deck chairs watching. That's about Sig Tau at Penn," Phoebe says.

Sig Tau is where I went that night with Plaid Shirt. Somehow even though I knew a lot of the stories in the book came from Penn, this hits me really hard. "Are you sure?"

"Oh, yeah. You know that senior Kelly Stahl? She had it done to her. She told me about it in Women's Studies. She wants people to know. She's really pissed. She was fooling around with this guy one night and the phone in his room rings, and a hand reaches in from the outside and answers it."

"That's so humiliating."

"See? That's just what I mean, though. No offense. But your gut reaction is to say it's so humiliating for her, not how terrible those schmucks at Sig Tau are. I think that's what I was talking about, some kind of societal conditioning we have. And that's like how women who are beaten blame themselves and don't want to tell people because they're embarrassed."

"And it's not just physical abuse, Phoebe, it's regular daily life too. We take all this shit from guys that we'd never accept from each other, you know what I mean? Because we think we somehow deserve it or we can't do any better. Or we think relationships should hurt, somehow, like it always has to be hard."

"Tell me about it," Phoebe says. "I know. Look at me and Chevs. How I let him treat me."

"He was so good to you in the beginning, Phoebs."

"I guess so. But I put up with a lot of shit for a long time. Stuff I never told anyone."

I wonder if "anyone" means me too, but I don't want to pry. She'll tell me when she's ready. "So what are we supposed to do about it?"

"What do you mean?" Phoebe says.

"We can sit here saying all of this, but some guys are good, or you hope they are, or you want to find one and just change him enough. And as stupid and hopeless as it is, I'm not ready to give up. But that's so weak."

"I don't think it's so weak. What are you supposed to do if you're

85

a straight woman? You spend your life waiting for the exception to the rule. If all men sucked or if we didn't think we could change them, there wouldn't be a problem in the first place. We'd all just give up and buy vibrators or something."

We both laugh.

"So this seems like the perfect time to ask what you're wearing on your big date," Phoebe says.

"Oh, yeah." I sigh and look at my watch. "I don't even want to go."

"Don't say that. Maybe he's the one good one."

"Yeah, maybe." I pour myself a cocktail.

9

★

i play winner

I wonder if I'll recognize Trey, but I do, right away. He's on time and he doesn't look so out of place, standing on the front steps of my high-rise. I watch him as I push through the turnstile; his hands are shoved in the pockets of his jeans. He's looking up at where my room might be. I like the strong look of his shoulders, the line of his neck. It's a relief to have an expectation met, to find something familiar and good. I hope he's relieved about me too. Maybe he's even pleasantly surprised. Phoebe made me wear a ribbed sweater that shows my body a little too much. I have lipstick in my back pocket to reapply.

"Hi," he says, smiling. "You look nice."

I notice that his eyes have shards of a greenish color, like moss, in them, that I haven't seen before. "So do you."

He looks down at his bucks. "All ready to go?"

"I think so."

We walk along the street between Highrise North and ATO. Someone throws a glow-in-the-dark Frisbee. It veers off, right in front of Trey. He catches it easily, then slices it back through the air, straight as paper.

At Backstreets, a bunch of guys in the back are playing Skee-Ball, air hockey, and darts. There's a container full of Blow Pops behind the bar. I circle my eyes around the room. "Vodka grapefruit?" Trey asks.

I nod.

"Shot too?"

"No thanks," I say. "Well, yeah, okay. And a Blow Pop."

I drink the shot right away so that I don't have to carry it around and then I chase it with a few licks from the Blow Pop. I wish I liked beer. That's the most portable thing. Trey drinks Bass ale.

For a while we watch people play games. I wonder if he's noticing that we aren't really talking, if he thinks he made a mistake maybe, taking out a college sophomore. I scan the room.

I'm actually pretty good at the game where you shoot these metal disks along this wooden surface covered in sawdust. You just push the disk firmly along the wooden tabletop in a straight line. It's a momentum thing. Most guys suck at it because they overshoot and the disk goes careening off the end of the shiny surface into a pile of sawdust at the edge. I feel like it's sexy to be good at something like this.

"Do you want to play?" I ask Trey. I point to the now empty table in a way I hope seems challenging and flirtatious.

"Sure."

We order second drinks and bring them with us. I shoot well. I imagine myself as a sexy girl with long hair, leaning over a pool table, announcing, "Yellow ball in the corner pocket," and not needing to look to be sure.

"Impressive," Trey says. Sure enough, when it's his turn, he overshoots. He looks a little frustrated when he picks the disk up off the floor. I watch more and more people fill up the bar and hear the familiar sound of lots of people getting drunk; it reminds me of peeking into the living room during my parents' dinner parties when I was little. I look closely at as many faces as I can. I don't know what my point is in bringing Trey here. I suppose I want to see Ryan, or I thought I did before, but right now it doesn't seem that simple, sort of like I'm wanting not to see him.

"So," Trey says, "another round?"

I wonder if he's wanting to get me drunk so that he can get the fooling around that didn't happen the last time we were together. Who knows? It tires my brain just trying to puzzle these things out without actually asking them.

Trey keeps talking about how he was a Sigma Chi in undergrad at Cornell and how he's met all the brothers here and they always try to get him to come to parties. Between shots, he tells me this story about when he was pledging: The older brothers made four of the pledges carry five kegs back to a beer distributor on purpose, so they would have to decide who would manage the fifth keg and how. Trey decided to throw it into the quarry. It seems like he's trying to show me how rebellious he is. I wonder why he's telling me this stuff at all. It was a long time ago; why does it matter? It seems like he's got something to prove, and I don't see why he has anything to prove to me; after all, he's in Wharton grad school. It's pathetic to me, that I try so hard myself, but when someone is trying with me, I get suspicious. Like it's undeserved or something.

Then I hear a voice say, "I play winner," and I feel my stomach turn over. *Calm yourself, Beck. It's not him. Breathe.*

Only it is him.

Trey makes his last shot.

"I've got winner," Ryan says, walking right over to us and refusing to take his eyes off me.

I can't look away. I have a million questions I want to see answers to, right there in his face.

"Well, you have her then," Trey says, handing him the shooter disk from the floor.

I hate that Trey doesn't know better, even though there's no way he could. He's giving me away without a fight. "Trey, I know him. This is Ryan." I watch them shake hands and put my hand on the side of the game table to steady myself. *Float like butterfly. Sting like bee.*

"Actually, Ryan, we don't have time for another game." I say what I wish Trey would have said. The last syllables crack; I feel my throat go dry. "We're going to Smokes."

"Well, congratulations," Ryan says. "To the winner." I know he's assessing Trey and I wonder what he thinks. Then I hate that I'm wondering.

"The game's all yours," Trey says. He puts his arm around me to guide me back to the table where our coats are still slung over the backs of the chairs. I'm happy that he's followed my lead, without asking questions. As we start to put our coats on, I hear Ryan yell my name from the other side of the room. Trey is trying to help me with my coat, but my arm keeps shaking, and I can't seem to get it into the sleeve. I just keep trying, ignoring Ryan and that he's coming closer and closer, until finally I give up on the coat. And then Ryan is standing beside us again.

"What's up?" Trey asks, nodding his head at Ryan just a little.

Ryan nods back but never takes his eyes off of me. "Rebecca, can I talk to you for a second before you go?" he says.

I can't believe this is happening. It feels like standing outside myself. I'm watching this play, and I've devised it, yet somehow I've lost control of it already. Again. Trey looks at me, as if to ask what I want to do.

"It'll only be a minute," I say, touching the shoulder of Trey's jacket lightly.

"I'll be waiting outside." He sounds a little pissed.

As I watch him walk away, I wonder briefly if I'll ever be the kind of person who would have walked out with him. And then I look back at Ryan, who's managing to look confident, even while just waiting. Something in the hang of his jeans alone makes me forget what wasn't good about sleeping with him.

"Okay, Ryan, I'm here. So talk, because I have to go." I finally manage to shrug the coat on.

"Is that your boyfriend?" Ryan asks, gesturing vaguely toward the door with his beer bottle, and emphasizing *that* just enough to make it mean. Then he reaches over and lifts my hair out from my collar. It feels too good, this little gesture, this little invasion.

"It's none of your business."

He lets a pause hang in the air. Then he touches the top of my hand lightly with two fingers. I let my hand slide off my hip and he picks it up and presses it into his own.

Stop, Beck. Pull your hand away. But I don't pull my hand away. I still feel something from this, something intense, like waves of nausea.

"I can't believe you're here," he says.

"Yeah. And?" A taste of his own medicine.

"I'm sorry about before. I totally fucked up. You have every right to be pissed. A lot of shit was going on with my parents and I just felt like I wasn't . . . but I am ready. I mean, I do want to be with you."

I shake my head. *No, no, no. I'm not that pathetic, Ryan. I'm too smart. I'm not going to let you fuck with me.* But no words come out.

"I mean it," Ryan says. "You have to think about this from my point of view. You're older. Smart. It's intimidating."

"I have to think of this from your point of view?" I jerk my hand away.

"Yeah—I mean, think about it. You left without saying good-bye."

"Ryan, please. You unbelievable shit. This—what you did to me—happened before we slept together. I liked you. I thought something was starting with us when we went to Smokes that night. And you took that and didn't think twice about trashing it, and now you want to be let off the hook?"

"It's not like that. We both messed up. But we can try right now."

"What are you going to say next, 'I'll call you'? Give me a little credit, Ryan. We didn't mess up. You did. I was straight with you and t wasn't easy. And you threw it in my face. I can't go back there like t didn't happen. Some things have consequences. Leave marks. You can't just order up another drink and pretend everything's okay."

"We messed up, Beck. If you liked me like you say you did, you didn't exactly show it. You could have called me."

"I did call you!"

"That one time. But now you act like it has to be me who calls, like there's this unwritten rule or something. But when you were with me, you were all tough and doing your whole feminist thing. It doesn't necessarily go together."

"Ryan, that's bullshit. I don't do a feminist 'thing' and it's not all that confusing. One person can only reach out so much. I did plenty of reaching out here. Too much. It's embarrassing."

"That's just what I mean. You supposedly like me but what you care about is how it looks, probably how I look, too, to your friends, being a freshman."

"Your being a freshman has nothing to do with it and you know it. Don't twist this around. Look, I have to go, Trey's waiting."

"If you're so into Trey, why are you standing here talking to me?"

"Because I'm an asshole," I call loudly over my shoulder as I push my way through the crowds and outside, where Trey is still waiting for me, hands shoved in his pockets, kicking something on the ground with the toe of his shoe. I wipe the hand Ryan touched on my jeans over and over.

"I'm sorry, Trey."

"It's okay. No, actually it wasn't. It was rude."

"I know. I'm really sorry. You're probably too mature to be dealing with all this bullshit."

"It has nothing to do with maturity. I shouldn't say that. It has nothing to do with how old either one of us is. I don't want to go to Smokes, Rebecca."

93

His Adam's apple jerks up and down when he talks, and his tone is so self-consciously steady that I can see exactly how upset he really is. I feel embarrassed for him and for myself too. I feel like a child.

"You don't want to go?" I ask.

"No, I don't. Why would I want to go to some undergrad bar so you can parade me around to your friends?"

"That's not fair. I really didn't know he would be there." But it is fair. It was my play, and I can't just throw up my hands, or I'm just like Ryan.

"Maybe we should just call it a night," Trey says.

"Are you sure? We could go somewhere else."

"Was that your boyfriend?"

"No. Did he seem like he was?"

"He seemed like he wanted something from you."

"No. He doesn't. And I don't want anything from him."

"You could have fooled me." Then Trey's voice softens. "Listen, I'll walk you to Smokes and then I'll catch a cab home, okay?"

"Okay. Thank you." I wonder if I have some kind of duty to salvage things, to make him want to see me again. But I feel too tired to, in the end.

Outside Smokes there's a pretty long line. He holds my hand and then drops it again. "Are you going to be all right?"

I feel like maybe I should start telling the truth. "Maybe not."

He smiles and gives me a hug. "Good-bye, Beck." Then he walks off toward Chestnut Street, raising his arm for a cab.

I stand outside of Smokes for a minute, watching him. Maybe he was the one good one. Maybe I'll never know.

10

★

old boys' network

Two cold, small hands press my eyes. "Guess who?"

"Hi, Susan," I say.

"How do you always know it's me?"

"We live together. I smell your shampoo."

"Oh. Well, I'm sooooo happy you're out tonight with us." She climbs on my back and puts her arms around me. When I don't hold on, she falls off. But she lands on her feet. "So what happened to Older Man?"

"The date ended," I say.

"Hmm, very mysterious."

"Are we going inside or am I going to stand here all night freezing, while you give me shit?"

"We're going in," Susan says.

The bouncer who's in love with Susan is working the door. He goes to Drexel. She peeks her head around the line so he sees her. He motions us to the front. "Hey, you guys," he says, "I saved your spot." Some people in the crowd groan. *"Quiet.* They were here before," he says. No one makes a peep after that. The Smokes bouncer is all-powerful. I feel bad about the cutting, but it's been a bad night. And it's really cold.

Susan and I go upstairs. The key to Smokes is having a booth. There are two ways to get one. Either you get there early (by 10:30 P.M.) or you make conversation with people at a booth until someone asks you to sit down. Then, as people leave to mingle, you call over your own friends to sit in the empty spots until it's just you and your friends. Plan A is out by the time we get to Smokes and I'm not in the mood to deal with Plan B. I ponder the merits of table vs. bar. Then I see Phoebe across the room. "Phoebe!" I yell, not caring when Susan gives me her embarrassed look. Phoebe is talking to Chevs, but I can see by the way her arms are folded across her chest that it's not going too well. She's got her book bag slung over her shoulder; she must have come from the library. Suddenly I feel a little guilty about all the work I know I have to do sometime.

"P! What's up?" I say as Chevs walks away.

Susan has drifted off and is surrounded by a big group of Tabard girls.

Phoebe rolls her eyes. "The usual. We should be friends. I should stop being so bitter. The same crap he always says when he's wasted."

"I'm sorry."

"Don't be. I've really gotten to a place where I am just not putting myself out there again. Or I'm working on it. So, how was the date? Is he here?"

I shake my head. We walk toward the booths and hover near one, waiting for someone to leave.

"Oh, God, did something bad happen?"

"I bumped into Ryan."

"Unbelievable."

"Not really. I took Trey to this bar that Ryan had told me he liked."

"Did you talk to him?"

"Yeah, I was pretty good. Not great, because I totally blew Trey off, but I actually told Ryan how I feel."

"And what did he say?"

"He said that it was partly my fault because I was never straight with him about my feelings and played games instead."

"Partly your fault? What an ass."

"I know. But, okay, Phoebe, you have to promise not to hate me and lose all respect for me."

"I promise."

"The thing is, I kind of want to believe him. I mean, I did play games. I could have been more direct. Maybe the game-playing scares him because of stuff that's happened with his parents."

"Wait a minute, Beck. If you want to give him another chance, that's fine. I won't lose respect for you, and I don't blame you. But don't let him turn this around to be about you and your supposed game-playing. You're not expected to put every single feeling out there at the very beginning of the relationship. That's weird. You don't sit there and say, 'Ooh, right now I'm wondering what our children would look like and writing my first name and your last together on a notebook,' even if you are. That's just, socially, not even normal. So don't let him twist this whole thing to make you out to be all coy or something. Because you aren't."

"You're right. I guess I just want him to have a good excuse."

"Well, like I said, you can always just give him another chance."

"And then watch him do the same thing all over again only with me looking and feeling like an even bigger idiot this time."

"Possibly, yeah. Probably."

"That sucks," I say.

Finally, a booth opens up. A waitress comes by for our drink orders. I have a vodka grapefruit, no shot. Phoebe was right before about my drinking a lot. I think about the lost night with Trey and try to count how many other lost nights, lost afternoons, there've been. But that's a tricky project, remembering blackouts, and I'm not sure why I think calculating the number is what I need to hammer it home. Isn't one dramatic enough? One whole night of lost time? We're always thinking how fast college is moving, the whole experience just dissipating before our eyes, and wanting to hold on, yet I'm just throwing nights away like they're nothing.

"Did you ever notice these pictures?" I say to Phoebe.

There are these photographs of athletes that line the walls of Smokes. To me they stand for the people who came before. Before Us, they were here. They were an Us. I hate to think of that, of the relentless way time keeps coming at you, especially at school where they march in a whole other class to replace you as soon as you graduate. I wish I could make it just stop for a second, so I could take a break, take inventory, document and categorize, but the "lasts" keep coming. The last time we went out as freshmen, the last high school keg party, the last day of summer.

I hate endings in general. I hated the end of spring break in high school. I just knew we'd never be together that way again. I hate the end of relationships, even bad relationships, just because it's the end of something. I actually remember sitting in the lounge cramming for my poetry exam freshman year and feeling a pang when my favorite highlighter dried up. I imagine these guys that I broke up with marrying someone else, making kids that wouldn't have been made if we'd stayed together.

It's too much to think about that, how the littlest thing—like a single phone message from Scott Childs—not only ended the relationship but possibly changed our lives. Like if I'd hung in, who knows, I could have turned out a different girl altogether. Maybe I've lost my soul mate, just because he got drunk and left a too intense message that he wanted to take back later and didn't even really mean. It's so serious, every ending, like what if I messed with fate? What if everything was going according to plan, but I resisted too much? What if Scott Childs's message was supposed to really move me and I was just too fucked up to be moved? Every ending makes me wonder about what I've lost.

"These pictures give me the creeps," Phoebe says, looking at a grainy black-and-white photograph of a guy in an old-fashioned sports costume, posed on a single knee with a medicine ball. It's feathered at the edges.

But that's not the one that stands out to me. "What about this one?" I say. It's a head shot, just above our booth. He's so handsome, but standoffish, it makes you almost have to brace yourself to look at him, makes you suck in air without thinking. His eyes have a sharpness that even in black and white says blue to me; his dark hair, cut in a flattop, emphasizes the squared jaw, the high cheekbones. I've thought about him at random times before, wondering who he is and why that picture was taken and what he's thinking about. He's someone who looks so impenetrable that, when he makes the smallest gesture of kindness—thanks you for the pen, offers you gum, holds the door—you stumble over yourself, forgetting all of the acts of kindness by the nice guys who came before. He probably drove his red-orange MG down Locust Walk to his Young Democrats meeting, his Friars Club meeting, squash practice. He breezed through the same halls we do, sang the same songs on the football field.

"It feels like he's listening to us, does that seem crazy?" I say. "We're sitting here waiting for more drinks, watching the hookups and the little fights, everything that's going to be gossip tomorrow. We're sitting here letting more and more time go by, and his time is over. It's as if he's saying, 'Look at me; look at the person I was once. All those moments slipped away so fast. If you're not careful, you become someone you never intended to be. And you can't go back.' —Hey, Phoebe, where's your book bag?"

She pulls the bag from under her seat.

"Can I borrow some paper?"

Phoebe takes out a spiral notebook, rips out a bunch of pages, and hands them to me. I pass some back to her. I reach in her bag for two pens and start drawing stick figures and smiley faces on all of the pages. Phoebe does too. Then I stand on the seat, reach over, and start covering up the photographs, one by one, pressing the ripped edges of the paper around the frames. No one seems to notice. I save the best for last and do it carefully and with relish, covering up those blue eyes, the eyes that see too much, know too much about all of our futures.

11

★

first run

By the time I get home it's after two-thirty. Maggie's asleep and Jane and Susan aren't home yet. I lie down on my bed and try to decide whether it's worth going out again. I'm tired, but I know I won't be able to sleep. I'm having terrible bed spins and they're worse when I close my eyes, like being blindfolded on a merry-go-round. I put a steadying foot on the floor and try to make it stop. In a sense I'm relieved not to have to listen to Jane and Susan replay the gossip of the night, something I usually look forward to. But I also feel so lonely, the kind of loneliness you don't even want to admit because then you make it real.

A part of me wants to call home and tell my parents that I miss them. I used to do that when I was little and I was visiting my grandmother in Buffalo. And once in a while my mom would say, "We wish we could give you a big hug." I don't know if she really meant it—maybe it was just something she said—but it meant everything to me. Even though I was a little kid, I had worries—not wearing the right clothes, looking weird because I was in all of the advanced groups in school, coming home to an empty house and having to protect myself against potential intruders using only a recorder. Just that one sentence from my mother used to make all the worries stop coming forward, folding onto each other like waves.

But whenever I think of those times, I remember camp too. Camp changed everything, and every time I think about it, it makes my stomach hurt and my chest feel heavy. I tell myself not to go there. I could go into the living room and watch a movie. I could make a mix tape. I could see if there are Twizzlers left, or cigarettes. But I can't help myself. I start remembering.

Every summer, I went to camp for two months. My parents thought one-monthers were crybabies who couldn't handle the full eight weeks away from home. "Maladjusted," my parents whispered to each other, while they told the crybabies' parents that only wanting to stay a month was perfectly normal.

That first summer, when I was nine, I was insanely homesick. I wrote letters to my parents and to each of my friends every day. We took these two-night sleepovers on dark islands where mosquitoes would buzz endlessly beside my ears. I'd cry all night with my sleeping bag bunched into my mouth so no one would hear. Lolly, our bunk counselor, who reeked of pot and giggled constantly, was unsympathetic.

My best friend defected when I wouldn't sneak into the boys' camp after a sing-along. But the worst was the night I got lost in the woods looking for the outhouse. I finally peed in my pants. Then, crying, I followed the light of the main cabin to get my bearings, stumbling over branches and scraping up my bare feet. I ran back down the hill to my bunk and hid my cotton Carter's under the mattress.

I couldn't wait for Parents' Day. I just wanted to hug my parents. We couldn't have candy at camp, but Parents' Day was an exception.

I had asked for my favorite foods: Heath bars and chocolate Hostess cupcakes. My mom had promised me a whole shopping bag full.

I couldn't sleep the night before. I switched off between scrunching up my eyes, and giving up and reading until the sun finally came up. Our parents were arriving right after breakfast. I put on my cleanest jeans and a pink, button-down shirt, rolling the sleeves three times like my father had shown me. "This is how the girls at Smith wear them," he'd said. I didn't even care that I had tray duty. As I scraped the orange plastic trays and the smell of garbage penetrated my nostrils, I thought, "My parents are coming!" and pictured them walking down the dirt road that connected the parking lot and the camp.

When our table met approval and the bell rang to signal the end of breakfast, I ran down the front steps to wait. I watched a crowd of parents come over the hill, but mine weren't there. Arm in arm, the other parents and kids strolled toward the bunks and the lake. Finally, when I couldn't take any more waiting, I ran down the dirt road. I almost smashed right into my parents.

They looked so perfect, my dad in his Ray•Bans and faded polo shirt, my mom in her washed-denim prairie skirt. I didn't even notice that they were empty-handed. They smiled, but I caught them looking at each other. I wrapped my arms around each one in turn. "I'm so happy to see you!" I said. "I missed you."

"We can tell." My dad's voice was pleasant but trying a little too hard. I saw his jaw clench. But I couldn't afford to pay attention.

We had a tour of the camp, a pottery demonstration, and a special lunch with make-your-own sundaes. It almost made me forget that instead of the treats I'd wanted, my mom had pulled a couple of rolls of Life Savers out of her skirt pocket. At the end of the day, I wanted to walk them to their car. They looked at each other again.

"You don't need to do that," my mother said.

"But I want to. What's wrong with that?"

My father was fixing something on his shoe.

"David, do you want to say something?" my mother asked.

"It's not necessary," my father said.

"What? Just say it!" I said.

My mother took over while my father fiddled with his shoe some more. "It's just that your father was concerned . . . well, we were concerned that this morning none of the other kids ran out to meet their parents the way you did."

"I missed you," I said, my voice breaking.

"We know, honey, and that's nice. But you were the only one. Little kids get homesick. You're growing up now. We want you to be happy at camp. We want you to get along with the other kids and—"

"I get it, Mom. I don't need to walk you to the car, I get it."

"We're sorry we didn't get the right snacks," said my dad.

"It doesn't matter."

When I got back to the cabin, I wrote in my diary that I would never again tell my parents I missed them. And I never did.

I pick up the phone and put it down again. But I don't know why I even do that much; there's no way I could call them at this hour anyway. The whole thing is a fantasy. Then I decide to go to Scott Childs's. I just want to feel taken care of. I just want to flop myself into someone's arms and be tired for a while. It's a little before three, so the escort service is still running. I put on sweats and sneakers and call an escort van to his place before I can change my mind.

I see Scott a lot still. For one thing, except for recently, I go to every Sigma Chi party. For another, he rooms off campus with Nate Rosen. We still flirt. He calls me Legs and asks me when I'm coming back to him. The last time I saw him he was studying in some obscure part of Van Pelt where I was trying to find some of the Jesse Jackson speeches I needed for my paper. I sat down with him for a while and he told me that he'd almost left because "the Bobbsey Twins" had shown up. That's what he calls Jane and Susan, "the Bobbsey Twins from hell." But then he stopped talking and touched my neck gently. "Your clasp is in front," he said. "Make a wish."

The escort van is packed and I start to lose courage. I wonder if everyone knows exactly what I'm doing. I go to the front door and pretend to be taking out keys and fitting them in the lock until the van pulls away. Then I go around to the side and throw gravel at Scott's window until he comes to the door in his boxers, rubbing his eyes. He lets me in without a word.

"Hi, Scott. I was just—I was at Smokes, and I was having these bedspins, so I thought—"

He just looks at me and smiles and pulls me up to him by the shoulders. He puts his arms around my waist and I put mine around his neck, like before. His mouth is warm and tastes like toothpaste and soda. I move in even closer and rub his shoulders. We stand there, kissing in the living room for a while, and he shakes his head and looks at me.

"What?" I ask.

"You are truly unbelievable, you know that?"

I hope in a good way. I lift my shirt over my head. Even though I am in sweats, I have a good bra on, black, lacy, and I pull my sweat-shirt around his back and pull him into the bedroom with it. I hope he's having fun because I don't want to be a tease. We fool around until I say stop when his hand is down my underwear, even though it still feels good, even though I suppose there's no reason not to have sex with him, now that I've already done it once. But I can't deal with that, like I couldn't with Trey. I just feel like once I start, I'll never stop, and like too much of me would be out there then, like I have to draw lines or I'll be lost. So I fall asleep, hoping for some good dreams.

When I wake up, it all comes back to me in bad-tasting pieces.

I threw rocks at Scott Childs's window. He obviously knew exactly what I wanted. I'm out of control, but I don't see any ending in sight. I can't imagine anything that would tie back together this package of me that's all unraveled now and bursting at the seams. Maybe he'll tell all his friends. How could he not tell people? This is exactly the kind of shit I know not to do; it's how you get a reputation, the kind of thing that makes *34th Street*. I slip on my clothes as quietly as I can and pray that the door won't creak. Then I pivot into the living room, ready for my next move. Only there, right in front of me, is Nate, wearing his trademark shit-eating grin.

"Go back to sleep, Nate," I say. My stomach is churning.

He opens the fridge, pulls out a carton of orange juice, and takes a slug as I scurry to the door.

"Let me get this straight," he says as I maneuver the latch. "Just for the record, was I dreaming, or did you throw rocks at our window at, like, four in the morning?"

"Later, Nate," I say, rolling my eyes for a nonexistent audience.

Outside, the sunshine seems way too bright. I start walking down Spruce Street and I see one of Scott's fraternity brothers leaving SDT. We look at each other and it's so obvious where we've both been, what we've both done. I have to smile, even though I still feel as sad as I did the night before, sadder even because being with Scott reminds me of the way things were between us before, almost normal, almost like a healthy boyfriend-and-girlfriend relationship, and I screwed that all up and I'm so far from the girl I was then, when we went on dates and he kissed me good-night and liked that I always ordered dessert. I feel like all my trademarks have been lost somehow, over just the past few days, and I'm floating around with nothing to identify me. I want to go back, to when I wasn't thinking so much, to when I could get the thoughts to stop just by inserting another fun activity, but I can't imagine what would bring me back there. The air smells so good, though, earthy and like leaves, and even though I feel confused, I'm still smiling and then I'm laughing. And then I just start running.

When I do, it's as if somehow things could possibly be okay, just because the air feels good and because even though I may not be able to sort things out, I can do things like this. I can kiss boys and I can be sad, and I can still wake up to a good-smelling morning. As I run, I let go of everything, my embarrassment, the flashbacks. My lungs feel like they're bleeding but I don't stop. I run right past the Quad, where Ryan lives, and it's so powerful to be able to run right past that, as if for this brief moment I can leave it all behind me. I lean my face up to the sun like I can't get close enough. I need to make it last.

As my feet hammer the ground over and over, I let something go, just a little. The sensation is familiar, the gaining of momentum, the breaking free, and I think back, flip through my memories like they're a box of crisp photographs, and then I remember. I was five years old, and my parents were driving me to my aunt's house for ten days because they were going to Florida. Lynda, the next-door neighbor, was staying with me. She was my friend, even though she was a few years older. She sat in the backseat of the station wagon, packed in with my colored mountains of toys, leaving me to my customary seat in the "way, way back."

While my parents were talking up front (the talking rapidly escalating to a fight), Lynda leaned over the back of her seat and suggested that I throw one of my toys out the window. "Can we get it back?" I asked.

"Sure. We'll swing by and get it back later. No problem."

I had a set of these colored plastic milk bottles. There was nothing even fun about those. One was orange with a white cap and one was yellow with brown. I think I had lost the third. Lynda rolled the window down and I threw them out. I looked back and saw the speck of orange grow invisible on the gray, blurry highway.

Then I pitched some red plastic coins from my Fisher-Price cash register. Then Raggedy Ann. Andy. The pink stuffed bear with the crusty mouth where I'd fed it chocolate ice cream. The miniature blackboard with the secret storage compartment for chalk and magnetic letters, canisters of Play-Doh that clanked as they hit the ground.

I glanced toward the front of the car. My parents were still arguing loudly about something. Lynda was staring out the side window, smothering her laughter with one hand. I stood on the backseat holding the backrest for balance. No one told me not to. I reached for beach balls. Books. A rubber ducky. Every time I threw something, I gained momentum. I hurled faster and faster. Something came over me then, a penetrating feeling of pure happiness, but with another layer too: somehow I knew it wouldn't last. I looked in the rearview mirror and saw a multicolored heap growing smaller and smaller. Then I turned back toward the front of the car. Not a single toy remained. Maybe I got a little worried then. "Lynda, are you sure we can get everything back?"

"Umm-hmm. Positive."

So I threw out my dad's Totes collapsible umbrella.

I don't know what made my parents suddenly snap to attention. The realization moment blurred into all of the swearing. The worst part of the whole crime was that black Totes umbrella. No one wanted to hear how we could get it all back. But no one explained why we couldn't. I remember the sharp, sudden swerve and the squeal of the tires as my father yanked the car to the side of the road without warning. I fell into the foot space below the seat and huddled there, holding my knees.

"Take her out and spank her," my father said to my mother.

111

I was so bad that my father couldn't even talk to me. During those moments of waiting for the spank, I thought I might throw up. My mom grabbed me out by my collar. It felt like the car was still moving a little. Cars on the highway were whooshing past without stopping, and the noise from each hurt my ears. No one talked. I heard our car's engine ticking every time the road got quiet, like little stones pinging against the fenders. Lynda was laughing and biting her lip as my mother smacked me on the ass over and over while I cried. I remember squirming, my head turned all the way back, watching that tightened hand approach again and again, too relentless and too hard. But my mother said later that it was more like a little tap. That it hurt her more.

Somehow, even as my feet pound the pavement over and over so satisfyingly, I know it won't last.

12

★

everything is fine

I circle past Chaucers and head home, panting.

As soon as I'm standing at the door to Highrise East, all of the bad stuff comes flooding back, just as I expected, starting with a paper I have to do for Art History tomorrow. Everyone is still asleep. I take a long shower and put on some clean sweats, and then I make a cup of instant coffee and lean out the window reading Sunday's Weddings section and smoking.

So many people in the Weddings met in college. I stare at the pictures, wondering how they could have found each other. I wish the little blurbs said something about that, like "They met at the library. He gave her his Psych notes. He wasn't her type at first but she hung in there and he grew on her." I just want some explanation for how things could ever possibly work out, how the right girl could ever like the right guy and know it and be satisfied.

Then I see it, a phone message for me: "3 A.M. Ryan called. He wanted us to try to find you. We said we didn't know where you were. Where the hell were you? He sounds psycho. Call him."

number 6 fumbles ★ Rachel Solar-Tuttle

I read it and reread it. He called me. Unsolicited this time. I find a giant Toblerone bar in the cabinet, wrap myself in a quilt, and press the *Ferris Bueller's Day Off* tape back into the VCR again. It's toward the end; Jennifer Grey is talking to Charlie Sheen in the police station. Even with the sound turned all the way down, I know what they're saying. I suck the triangles of chocolate and fall asleep before Ferris makes it safely home.

When I wake up, it's afternoon. Susan and Jane and Maggie are going to study at Rosengarten. "Come with us," Susan says.

"Who took this message?" I ask her.

"Jane did."

"Jane, what did he sound like?"

"I don't know. Maybe drunk, I'm not sure."

"That's helpful. What did he say exactly?"

"I wrote it all down, Beck!" Jane wails.

I don't know why I'm giving her this third-degree. Do I hope he had offered the truth, or something somehow revealing to my roommate at 3 A.M.?

"Beck, I think you should come with us," Susan says. "Not sit here all day pining or whatever."

"I'm not pining, Susan. I'm tired. Maybe I'll see you there later."

"Beck, you are pining," Maggie says. "And it seems like you aren't doing any work."

"Maggie, how do you know what I'm doing? I've always done things at the last minute. You've just never lived with me before. And I get all A's."

"She does, Maggie," Susan says.

Susan's an English major too. My papers are always getting read aloud in our classes. I actually do all the reading and everything, and I've never handed in a paper late. I have a formula for papers:

(1) At around midnight, the night before, write down the first highly provocative idea that comes to mind (e.g., "In book X, food as a symbol of nurturing is turned on its head. Food symbolizes danger"). (2) Thumb through the book and support it with a million examples in chronological order. You can always find examples to support anything. It's all about how you spin them. (3) End with another provocative suggestion. I keep waiting for the rest of my friends to figure out how easy this is.

My roommates all leave. I pull out my Art History book, but nothing comes to me. We have to analyze a single piece of work by one of the artists in the group we've just finished studying. It's only a five-pager anyway. I put the book down and call Phoebe.

"What are you doing?" I ask her.

"Thinking that I should go to the library and not wanting to."

"Tell me about it. Do you want to go to the White Dog?"

Mostly professors and grad students go to the White Dog, but we go sometimes for special occasions. The last time I was there was Parents' Weekend. My parents had decided not to come, so Phoebe and her dad had adopted me.

"Great idea," Phoebe says. "I need an hour, though. I have to shower and everything."

"I'll meet you outside," I say, thinking how I don't want to be alone for the hour.

I change into a soft cardigan and my good jeans and tie a scarf through my belt loops. Then I sit down on my floor and call Ryan.

"Yeah?" he answers on the first ring like he was waiting for someone else.

"It's Rebecca. I'm calling you back."

"You what?"

It's like he doesn't even remember that he called me. My palms start sweating.

"I'm calling you back. I got a message from you last night. Is now a good time?"

"Actually it's not."

"Oh. Okay. Well, do you want to call me later or something?"

"Yeah, yeah. I'll call you later. Or I'll see you around."

"Fuck you!" I scream as I put down the phone. "Fuck, fuck, fuck!" I kick the wall until my toe throbs. He called me. He asked me to call him back. And yet he manages to make me feel like such a loser. What was he doing that was so important? And he'll see me around? What the fuck is that? I had something when he left me that message, and now I'm back the way things were before, with nothing. I feel so completely humiliated. I'm so glad that my roommates aren't here, because I really start to bawl then. I can't move; I'm still sitting right by the phone and I pick it up and call my parents without even thinking about why.

But as soon as the phone starts to ring, I do know why. I want them to pick up so badly. I want to say "Mommy" even though I haven't called her that in years. I don't even really call her Mom anymore. I want her to hug me tight, so I don't have to think about even breathing. I want to go back to being a kid again, to a day when I was sick and had a dangerously high temperature and she made soup for me and my dad brought me home Snoopy sheets.

"Hello?" Her voice sounds a little pinched; I feel right away that what I want to happen isn't going to, that I should just hang up the phone. But still I try.

"Hi, Mom." I light a cigarette and exhale away from the phone so she can't hear. My lip is trembling.

"Hi, honey. We haven't heard from you in a while."

"I know." I wipe my eyes but new tears fall back out right away. I'm sure she must be able to hear me, or to know somehow. I'm sure she'll ask me what's wrong. And then I can let it all pour out of me and she'll tell me how she felt the same way once, when she was in college, when she was my age.

"How's school?"

How could she ask me something like that? How's school? "It's fine."

"What happened with that paper?"

"What paper?"

"The Whitman one? Did you redo it?"

"I didn't have time to redo it, Mom. It was due the day after I talked to you."

"The day after we talked? But it sounded like you only had an idea for that paper. Oh, honey. You can't do things at Penn all last-minute the way you did in high school."

"Mom, isn't there anything else you want to ask me?" I'm watching the tears drip onto the cover of my journal now, not even trying to stop them.

"Something I want to ask you? I don't know what you mean, honey."

"Remember that time when I was little and I had a fever and you made soup for me?"

"I think so. I'm not sure. Sometimes you pretended to be sick. One time I remember the nurse figured it out and called me in to talk about why you were faking it." She laughs.

"Forget it. That's not what I was asking. I have to go. Tell Dad I say hi."

"What is going on, Beck? Is something the matter? Are you sick now?"

"No. I'm fine. It was stupid. I have to go. I'm meeting somebody."

"I'm worried about you, Rebecca. If you're sick, you should go to Student Health."

*   *   *

I'm back there again, in my mother's station wagon. I got into an accident, so my car's in the shop. My mother is driving me home from the SATs on her way back from the dry cleaner's. I'm still gripping my five sharpened number two pencils. I flip my sunglasses down from the top of my head and look out the window.

"So, how do you think you did?"

"I don't know. Okay, I guess. I tried." In truth, I have no idea. There were a lot of things I wasn't 100 percent sure about—questions that could have gone either way. Right now I'm just so relieved that it's over. I turn the knob on the radio, until the Beastie Boys' "Brass Monkey" comes through. Loud.

"Okay you guess?" My mother snaps the radio off.

I exhale so my bangs blow up and flop back down again. My mother takes a turn too sharply, and all the dry-cleaning bags slide across the seat and mound up in the foot space, crinkling.

"I said I tried. But I'm not sure it went too well." I imagine her turning toward me, telling me that no matter how I did, I'd still be her daughter and she'd still love me the same way, and then asking me if I want to go to Buttrick's for butter-crunch ice cream cones, like we did after doctor's appointments when I was little. But instead I see the veins on her neck bulge. She tightens her grip on the wheel.

"Why do you think you couldn't get it together, Rebecca?" she asks, spitting out the words.

At that moment, I picture myself grabbing the wheel, pulling the car out of control, killing us both. "I don't know, Mother." I stare straight ahead. "I guess I just decided to fuck up today."

I glance at her in time to see her raise her hand to hit me. She watches me catch her in motion and says nothing, just lowers her hand so slowly and reluctantly there's no mistaking what I've seen.

When my scores come back, they're in the ninety-fifth percentile. Only Trudie Wexler has done better, and she has anorexia and would have to defer Yale anyway if she got in early. I am redeemed again.

It's almost time to meet Phoebe. I walk into the bathroom and look in the mirror. My eyes are red and they seem deeper than before, somehow. They're ringed with dark purple circles. I look like a ghost. I feel like I don't even know this girl. I splash some water on my face and take out a compact. I cover the circles and the redness around my nose. Then I powder everything and line my eyes with blue liner. I look at the ceiling and try to stop crying so I can put on mascara. I brush my lip gloss on, holding up my elbow with my other hand to stop the brush from shaking. I rub some blush into the apples of my cheeks. Paint myself back into a happy girl, so I can walk around campus and look like I'm someone who knows what she's doing, as usual. I step into the elevator and people smile at me like I'm real.

"So Ryan called last night," I say to Phoebe as we walk over the bridge.

"Are you kidding me? What did he say?"

"He called at three in the morning, and I had gone over to Scott Childs's."

Phoebe shoots me a look.

"I know, I know. It was a stupid thing to do. I felt like I needed that, though."

"Are you okay?" Phoebe asks.

"Not really. I didn't sleep with him. But I almost don't know why I didn't."

"It's good that you didn't. I know after your first time, it just feels like there's never any reason not to. But you have to protect yourself."

"My reputation?"

"No. I don't even believe in that. I hate how a guy sleeps with women and he's a legend, and a girl does it for exactly the same reasons and she's a slut. But you have to protect yourself. On the outside you're probably all cool with the idea of sex, and it feels like it's a need like anything else that you have every right to satisfy. But there's a nugget inside of you that will be sad and regretful. I'm telling you this from experience because I've learned the hard way. Even if you only mean for it to be sex and nothing more. It's like cotton candy. And after the night is over, those layers of pink sugar just unravel and unravel until you're left standing there holding a dirty wet stick. Does that make any sense?"

"Yeah, I get it. But what is it about sex more than any other kind of fooling around that makes you feel that way? You were the one who said that sex isn't such a big deal and that only society made you feel like it was supposed to be so transforming or something."

"I don't know," Phoebe says. "Maybe that's it, that society makes such a big deal out of it and uses that to measure whether you're a slut, so somehow it makes you feel trashy and used. Or maybe it's the act itself, the way you're uncovered. Maybe it's because we're always taught that if we do it, we're supposed to love the person, so when we do it without love, we almost start to feel like it's there, almost to make it be there, so it's okay in our heads."

"I keep thinking about Laura Lacosta."

"Oh, I know. That's exactly what I mean. She put herself so out there."

Laura was seeing Fleet McCauley for a while. At a party one night when everyone was sitting around upstairs listening to music and smoking cigarettes and chewing, we ended up in a crazy shaving-cream-and-deodorant-fight. Tasha squirted Fleet on the face with shaving cream and said, "How's that for a role reversal?" When everybody laughed but us, Tasha told us that Laura had once told Fleet to "pull out and come on my face." All ten people in the room knew then, including me, knew this totally personal, humiliating thing, and knew that everyone else was making fun of it. My relationship with Laura is just a "Hello" if we see each other on the Walk. But every time I see her, I know.

13

★

trusts

At the White Dog, we sit at a little table beside the front window and order Bloody Marys. The back part of the restaurant is fancier, with white tablecloths and silver, but I like it here even more, the small, round wooden tables and the light pouring in through the lace curtains and all the action around the bar where everyone reads newspapers and talks to each other. Our Bloody Marys come with clumps of horseradish and black pepper and big stalks of celery. We finish those before we decide what we want to eat, so we order two more. We light cigarettes. Then we both order the challah French toast with almond orange sauce. Pretty soon, I'm feeling nice and buzzed.

There's something that's so much fun about drinking during the day, much more so than on a to-be-expected Friday or Saturday night or even a Thursday night, which is actually usually the best night of the week here. There's something so spur-of-the-moment and almost weird about drinking when every library on campus is full of people. A lot of times Phoebe and I go out to Smokes or Palladium midday or on a Sunday night just because it's so different, taboo almost, and therefore

little bad-girl festive. Sometimes we come straight from the library with
ur books, just to have a drink or two, and end up involved in something
ompletely insane, like popping someone's codeine pills on the flight
eck or sitting around listening to some tape someone found of "Video
illed the Radio Star." It seems so quintessentially college, somehow;
/hen else are you going to be drunk in the middle of the day or party-
ıg with complete randoms on a Sunday night? I like that.

"The Bloody Marys are sooo delicious," Phoebe says to the
artender.

"Glad you like them," he says. "You'll have to try my pink
ɔmonades."

"Pink lemonades?" Phoebe asks.

"It's my special blend."

He puts citron vodka into two jam-jar glasses and then picks
p various unrecognizable liquor bottles and pours in a few drops from
ach along with a few shakes of cranberry juice. Phoebe and I finish
ur Bloody Marys, and he swoops them off the table and replaces them
/ith the pink lemonades. I can barely taste the liquor. It's like alcoholic
ˈountry Time. We gulp them down and order two more. Our food arrives.
Ve've lost our reserve and we butter the French toast like crazy and
's so delicious. By now it's gotten really crowded, and these two guys
/ho seem like they may go to the law school—they look older, wear
iifferent clothes, not the folded-baseball-hat fraternity-boy uniform, and
ley have huge book bags—sit down at the table right next to ours. My
hair back is almost touching one of theirs. Once they're sitting, Phoebe
; facing the other one, and I can tell she's peeking over my head.

"Cute," she says.

I try not to turn around.

"Do you mind putting this on the window ledge for me?" one of
lem asks, tapping me on the shoulder. "There's no room on our
ɪble for it."

125

"No problem," I say. The book is called *Wills, Trusts, and Estates*. It's red and thick as a dictionary. "Looks interesting."

"I thought it would be. Learning about how things pass to the next generations, how you make what happens at your death conform to what your true intent is. The professor's great. But actually it's killing me. We just took our mid-term."

Phoebe chuckles.

"I think 'looks interesting' was facetious, sport," his friend says. "Forgive him; he's a little high-strung."

"Have a pink lemonade," I say. "Trust us."

"Can we buy you guys another too? To thank you for baby-sitting Carlton's big book. I'm James, by the way."

"Rebecca. And this is Phoebe. Another drink would be cool."

He signals the waiter, and Phoebe and I vacuum up the rest of our pink lemonades. Carlton and James look at us and raise their glasses, so I turn and we raise ours too. "Do you mind if we smoke?" I ask, pulling the ashtray to the center of the table.

"Not at all," James says, producing an antique-looking silver Zippo and getting up to light our cigarettes. "Mmm. Parliaments. Interesting choice."

"Don't start with me," I say. "It's been a long week."

He laughs and goes back to his table, where he and Carlton begin talking in hushed tones. I can only imagine how much those two are dying to hook up with a couple of little sophomore under-grads. I bet the law school girls give them a run for their money and Phoebe and I look young—like easy prey. Oh, well. The drinks are free. And they are sort of hot.

"Why don't you pull over a couple of chairs?" James finally says.

"Oh, be serious," Phoebe says. "It's way too crowded over there. Besides"—she puts her AmEx card on the table without glancing at the bill, and the waitress scoops it up—"we were just leaving."

"Why don't you come with us then? We were just leaving too." James flags the waitress then, exactly the way Phoebe did. The waitress chuckles. "We're going to Cavanaugh's."

Cavanaugh's is this big, characterless, cheesy sports bar just off campus, near these run-down apartments called Hamilton Court where a lot of juniors and seniors live. It has no personality, but you can dance there sometimes, and you can get drinks pretty quickly because the bar is huge and there are always lots of bartenders. "What are you going to Cavanaugh's in the middle of a Tuesday for?"

"Why not? College soccer game," Carlton says.

"So we get to sit around watching you watch soccer? Mmmm, so appealing," I say.

"We promise not to concentrate on the game," James says. Carlton shoots him a look. "Much. And it's our treat, of course."

"Is he your spokesman or something?" I ask Carlton. He looks at the ground.

"You're treating to all the drinks?" Phoebe asks. " 'Cause we can really put 'em away."

"I'm sure," James says, smiling.

I look at Phoebe. "Okay," she finally says, "let's go."

At first, Phoebe and I walk together up Walnut Street, sort of behind Carlton and James. Then somehow we end up all paired off, so I walk with Carlton the rest of the way. Actually, I stumble a little. He holds my elbow.

"I've always wanted to go to law school," I say.

"Oh, yeah?" Carlton says. "Why's that?"

"What else are you going to do with a degree in English to make money? And I don't want to be one of those wives who earns nothing and then has no spending power in the relationship."

"Well, that's forward-thinking of you. But law school blows.

People are still dropping like flies, even though it's our second year."

"But you're out on a Tuesday, going to White Dog, watching your game, looking for a little undergrad booty. That seems pretty fun," I say.

"I can't believe you just said that. We were not 'looking for booty.'"

"Right."

"You're pretty funny, though." Carlton laughs.

"Thanks."

"Do you have ID?" Carlton asks.

"Do you?"

"I'm twenty-four. I don't need ID."

"Well, la-di-da. Of course I have ID. What do you think I do at this school, sit around playing Boggle?"

He laughs again.

I hand him my ID. "See. It's real too. And I'm twenty-eight. Older than you."

"This thing actually works?"

"Of course it works. It's a real Maryland license. We had this exchange student from Sweden one year, Elspeth. And she was completely boy crazy and had very broken English. So I helped her write all of her love letters to these guys we would meet downtown when my mom sent us to the aquarium and stuff. She did a semester at Maryland, and when she was done, she sent me her driver's license."

"That's unbelievable. You don't look a thing like her. And it's expired. And people buy that you're twenty-eight?"

"They buy it enough to let me in everywhere. I've had it since high school and I've never had a problem." I kiss Elspeth's laminated face to show my gratitude.

Carlton laughs.

At this point we're at the door to Cavanaugh's, so I flash my ID and we're in. "See?" I say. The place is pretty empty and we settle into seats at the bar. Near the TV, I notice.

"What would you like to drink, Rebecca?"

"You can call me Beck."

"Okay, Beck. Wait a sec. Oh my god! You're Beck! You're Beck!" Carlton is screaming now.

"What are you talking about?" I say.

"Hartley," he yells to James, who seems to be embroiled in some kind of high-level debate with Phoebe. "This is Trey's Beck!"

"Oh my god," I say.

"Oh, man!" Carlton says. "You're a junior?"

"Sophomore." I could just stand up and leave right now. I count how many steps I'd have to take to get from my barstool to the door.

"He told us you were a junior! He was totally into you and you blew him off. He's gonna die when he hears I'm out with you."

"You're not out with me. I'm out with Phoebe and we bumped into you. How do you know Trey anyway?"

"We went to high school together. We're best buds. He almost came with us today, actually. That would've been hysterical. He's never going to believe this."

"Yeah—that we're actually out with The Hoover," James says.

"Dude!" Carlton says, shushing him.

But I'd already heard. "The Hoover? What the hell is The Hoover?"

"You heard me wrong," James says.

"Don't insult our intelligence," Phoebe says, "I heard it too."

The bartender asks for our order. "Two shots of Absolut and two Absolut and grapefruits," Phoebe says. Clearly we're going the expensive route. Carlton and James order Rolling Rocks.

"Well, the game's about to start," Carlton says.

"Fuck you, Carlton," Phoebe says, making his name sound like the most stupid thing in the world. "What's The Hoover? What are you talking about? Obviously it's some kind of insult."

"Actually, it's a compliment," says James. Carlton stares into his beer. "Let's just say that Carlton's friend found you to be, uh, extremely talented."

"What?" Phoebe says.

"Uh, how can I put this delicately? Extremely talented with your mouth," James says.

"What? Trey did not say that! Like I gave him a blow job or something? Yeah, right. We barely did anything."

Carlton and James look at each other.

"Why do all of you feel the need to lie like that? It's so pitiful. You know, if it were true, I'd admit it. I'm sick of the double standard where you run around bragging and we act all embarrassed or something. The thing that pisses me off is that he felt the need to fucking lie about it. Trey was embarrassed because we bumped into someone I—used to date and I stopped paying attention to Trey. So he makes up all this bullshit—"

"Calm down," Carlton says.

"Don't patronize her," Phoebe says.

"Oh, we wouldn't dare," says James.

"Let's get out of here," Phoebe says.

We suck down the drinks.

"Girls, girls. C'mon. There's no need to overreact. We were having such a nice time. Relax. Stay awhile. Let's watch the game."

"Dream on," I say. "And would you give Trey a message for me? Tell him I give an amazing blow job. Too bad he'll never know."

"Later, much," Phoebe says. And we leave.

the end of an era

It was light when we went into Cavanaugh's but now it's starting to get dusky out. "I can't believe that," Phoebe says, "except that I totally can."

"I know. Jerks."

"You were great, though. So was that true?"

"What?"

"Do you really give an amazing blow job?"

"I don't know. I've never given one. I always felt like that comes after sex, like it's even more personal."

"Me too."

"But in boarding school my proctor showed me how on a half a Fudgsicle."

Phoebe laughs.

"Do you want to stay out? I don't feel like going home yet. Maybe people will be at Smokes."

"Okay," Phoebe says.

Smokes is pretty crowded, especially for a Tuesday night. We can't get a booth but we get a table near the back.

"Are you still upset about the thing with Trey?" Phoebe asks.

"Sort of. But I actually feel kind of bad for him. He seemed like a nice guy and he must be pretty insecure to lash out like that. But still, you know, I thought about maybe calling him or something and now I never could."

"Yeah, that sucks."

"Is it something about me that makes me get involved with guys who lie? First Ryan and now this. Two is a pattern," I say.

"Two is not a pattern. And it has nothing to do with you. It has to do with them. Maybe it's some kind of genetic flaw."

"Maybe."

"Maybe Ryan had a good reason for lying, though. Maybe he's right and you are intimidating. I could see that making him want to lie about his age and making him hesitant about calling, even if he said he would."

"Intimidating how, though? It's not like I walk around with my GPA tattooed on my forehead or anything. And everyone at this school is pretty smart anyway."

"But you're confident and attractive and witty and sarcastic. That could be intimidating. Not that you should care, or anything. I'm just looking for some kind of explanation."

"Confident? Ha. Are you nuts? I'm a loser chasing after some freshman who's so not interested in me and drowning all my sorrows in vodka."

"C'mon. Anyway, like I said, even if some guy is intimidated by you, you can't let it change you. I did that with Chevs sometimes. I kind of—I don't know—dumbed down. Let him think there was stuff I needed help with. And look what good that did me. I acted a little needy and he still ran away screaming. I think the point is just to act the way you want to and wait for someone who can deal with it."

"But we could be waiting forever. And college is the best place in your life for meeting appropriate guys."

"Who said that? Your mother?"

"Of course."

"Didn't she also say that good friends come and go but a good transcript lasts forever? And that people who use *party* as a verb sound like retards?"

"Oh, shit," I say.

"What?"

"I just remembered, we're getting our Am Lit papers back tomorrow. The one my mother had a fit about."

"So what did you end up doing it on?"

"A comparison on Whitman poetry and Jesse Jackson speeches. Barbaric yawps."

"That's brave."

"So you think it's stupid too?"

"No, I think it's really interesting. It's just brave because of who she is."

"The professor?"

"Right."

"Who is she?"

"Oh, God," Phoebe says. "You don't know?"

"Tell me."

"She's a famous Whitmanian scholar."

"Holy shit! No!"

"Oh my God. I'm so sorry. I thought you knew. Her books are in that special display case in the library."

"Books? Meaning more than one? I am dead. So dead. Could my life possibly suck any more?"

"Maybe she'll love it. I'm sure it was great."

"Yeah, right. She's going to be like, 'Hello, Emperor, you're stark fucking naked!' And I have an Art History paper due tomorrow."

"Should we get going then?"

"No. I don't want to think about it now. Let's have another drink."

"Are you sure?"

The people at the bar watching TV let out a huge roar.

"Yeah, I'm sure."

Phoebe has a fresh pack of cigarettes and she taps them against the back of her hand while we wait for our drinks to come, then rips off the foil covering in front. There's this ritual, where you count across the cigarettes in a new pack until you get to the number of letters in the first name of whoever you like. So if you like Daniel, you count six cigarettes in, for D-A-N-I-E-L. And then you turn that cigarette over and smoke it last. That way, you'll end up with Daniel. "Which one should we turn over?" Phoebe asks. I turn over the fourth cigarette in. I can't help myself.

"You do not seriously want to end up with Ryan," Phoebe says, lighting the turned-over cigarette so my wish won't come true.

"Oh my God, Phoebe. Um, two, no, three o'clock." I'm not so great with the clock thing yet. I learned on a digital.

"The hot black guy in the red flannel?"

"You think he's hot? He's Ryan's best friend. I met him with Ryan that first night. Jared. I wonder if Ryan's here."

"Well, Jared's coming over."

"No way."

"Way. He's making a beeline right for—"

"Hi, Jared."

"Rebecca, hi."

"You remember my name? How flattering. This is Phoebe."

"Phoebe." He holds out his hand. I wouldn't call it manicured, but it's the hand of someone who's never once raked leaves. "Pleasure to meet you. Mind if I sit down?"

"Not at all," I say. "Where's the rest of your posse?"

"You mean Ryan?"

"Ahh, excuse me," Phoebe says, "I have to run to the women's room."

"Is Ryan all you have for a posse? That can't be good. Not what I'd call a reliable posse."

"Yeah, about that. You've gotta give Ryan a chance. Or I think you should."

"Why are you always defending him?" I ask.

"Look, I know he can be a jerk, but he's my best friend. And he's fundamentally a good guy. He has a good heart. He's just been through a lot of shit. He could use something—I don't know, good, steadying, in his life. We all think you're the best thing that's ever happened to him."

"You sound like you've taken a campus-wide survey," I say.

"Well, me and Bob think so."

"Bob?"

"Bob Chan. One of our other roommates. The rest of the posse. He hooked us up with the four-room quad."

"Who's the fourth?"

"Mondavi. The psycho chair-thrower."

So there actually was a Mondavi. Amazing. One true thing. "And why have you undertaken this little project?"

"No one thinks Diana's good for him. She treats him like shit, and we're all sick of seeing her around. Ryan needs some help finding the right kind of woman. And I said that night at New Deck, I thought you were cool as shit—"

"Diana?"

"Oh, shit, did he not tell you about her?"

"Diana?"

"He definitely told us he was going to. Well, it's over, anyway, I mean really over. She's transferring to Hobart. And I think he really wants another chance with you; he just doesn't know how to ask.

Plus, you know he's been in the hospital. He went home to the city with a stomach flu."

Do not get sucked in. Do not get sucked in. "When? I saw him at Backstreets last night!"

"Yeah, he told us. Are you seeing that guy you were with? Ryan said he was kind of a dork."

"Trey is so not a dork. He's a first-year at Wharton grad." So Ryan clearly must have been jealous.

"Anyway, we all took Ryan to HUP this morning. Viral infection. They said he should be home where he can get some real rest."

"Well, as Ryan would say, 'Whatever.' You know, I fucking hate that expression. It's dismissive; it's condescending; it avoids having to actually deal with anything."

"I'll make a note," Jared says.

"Tell him if he wants something from me to tell me himself, not send some fucking emissary to do his dirty work."

"But I'm not—"

"Whatever," I say. "See how good it feels? I gotta go find my friend."

I get up and leave Jared sitting alone at our table. Then I walk around looking for Phoebe, only I don't see her anywhere. So Ryan had a girlfriend when we slept together. Perfect. He manages to take something horrible and make it worse. I wish I could get my first time back.

I check the bathroom. There's a half door in front that keeps people on the outside from seeing in when the bathroom door is open. When I get past that, I hear crying, not hysterical sobbing, but soft, real crying. I know it's Phoebe. I open the door. Phoebe and Chevs are standing there. He's holding her, rocking her back and forth, and she's crying over his shoulder. They look so right together, like movie stars or something. I can't believe that this is the same guy who acted like such a jerk. Phoebe sees me and smiles a little. I walk quietly away.

It's getting late and I have that paper to do, so I decide to go home. I know that Chevs will make sure that Phoebe gets back okay. It's strange, though, as I head out, something in the air starts to change. People seem to be buzzing around really fast or something, heading toward the back of the bar.

Then when I get to the door, someone unfamiliar asks me for my ID. "Why are you asking me for ID now?" I say. "I'm leaving."

"Because I'm from the Liquor Control Board. And I need to see a valid driver's license, please."

My blood starts to buzz and I'm shaking as I reach in my pocket and take out Elspeth's license, trying to look casual. I know how this works. He asks me questions about my ID. I've memorized the answers. I just have to stay calm. Meanwhile, the place is frozen now, with a whole line of people behind me waiting to meet the same fate.

"This is expired."

"I know. I don't drive anymore, so—"

"What's your address, Ms.—"

"Elspeth," I say. "Smith dormitory. University of Maryland. College Park, Maryland, 20742." Thank God I've practiced that address until I got it down.

"And what's your sign, Elspeth?"

I had heard they might try that one. "Cancer."

"Very nice," the LCB guy says, still holding my ID.

"Can I go now, sir?"

"Just one more. When did you graduate from high school?"

Shit. Between the pressure of the moment and my total and utter fear and hatred of math, I can't figure this out to save my life. The pause is way too long.

"Oh, God, um. I don't know. Um. It was so long ago, um—"

"Step inside, miss. And wait."

"You're taking my ID?"

"Yeah, I'm taking your ID. Now step aside!"

I notice, while I stand there completely humiliated, that he takes each confiscated ID and puts them in a big stack without marking whose is whose. I stand there for a long time while he goes through the process with about a hundred people, letting those who pass the test out into the night and lining the others up with me. I don't see Phoebe, though. I pray that Chevs took her out the back door.

Then someone taps me on the shoulder. It's Jared.

"Oh, God, you're still here?" I say.

"Yeah. And I am so fucked."

"What did you give them?"

"I have this passport from some Nigerian guy in my Filmmaking class. And they took it! He'll probably never be able to leave the country."

"I think you just say it was lost and you can get another one. He could have been mugged or something."

"Yeah, I guess so," he says.

"You take Filmmaking? I'm dying to take that class."

"All of you in line, shut the fuck up!" the LCB guy says. "This is going to be a long night, and the only way you're going to get through it is by shutting up and following directions."

"Follow my lead, Jared," I say out of the corner of my mouth.

I've done two things tonight that qualify as illegal. One, I have been in possession of a fake ID. Two, I've been drinking. The thing is, though, since they've put the fake IDs in a stack without identifying whose is whose (at least, as far as I can tell), they can't nail me for having the fake ID. And unless they do some kind of Breathalyzer, and I don't see any equipment for one (not that I actually know what Breathalyzer equipment would look like), they can't prove that I've been drinking. Fortunately, the scariness of the situation has sobered me up too.

It takes about an hour for the LCB to go through the entire bar's worth of IDs. It's sort of funny how everything always seems to move so fast, too fast, except this; the hour creeps along, feels like four. They keep yelling at us to be quiet. I'm tired. It's after two o'clock by the time they've rounded up all of the violators. They take us downstairs, separate anyone who seems to know anyone else, and put us all into booths where we wait some more as they walk from table to table. My pulse is jumping all around my body, making my feet shake, then my hands. Jared gets put in the booth behind mine. I look around again to make sure Phoebe's not here. She's not.

A few seniors who actually are twenty-one but just have duplicate licenses (the kind of replacement licenses you get if your wallet is lost or stolen, but which are also the easiest to fake) are getting pissed. "My father is head of litigation at Wolf, Block," one of them says, smacking her gum. "You are so going to pay for this."

"I don't care if your father's the king of England," the LCB guy says. But he does her booth first.

They walk from booth to booth asking all of these questions, getting real licenses, writing down information. Only the duplicate-license girls are allowed to leave.

By the time they get to me, I'm completely sober. It's a different officer from the one at the door. Plus, I was the first one busted, so even if it were the door guy, he probably wouldn't remember me anyway. In spite of all this, I almost feel too scared to activate my plan. But then I just think of my parents: "Hi, guys, sorry to bother you. Listen, I realize that when you said 'get involved with the law,' you actually meant, you know, law school, but—" There's no way. This just can't happen. It's not an option. "Sir," I say when they ask for my license, "I don't think I should be here. I didn't drink and I didn't show a fake ID." My insides are screaming. I can barely hear myself talk.

"So how did you get into the bar?"

"I was with a big group of friends. I didn't know they carded you to get in. I thought you only got carded when you drank. I wasn't even paying attention at the door. I was studying all night and I was really tired. They must not have seen me in the group I was in. And all I've had tonight is grapefruit juice."

"Well, you should know that we've got the equipment to do a Breathalyzer, so you will be tested."

But I still don't see any sign of the equipment he's talking about. "That's fine with me. If I could be tested sooner rather than later, I'd really appreciate it. I have an exam tomorrow. And I haven't done anything wrong."

"Hold your horses." He walks away for a moment and consults with someone else.

A few minutes later, he returns to my table. "All right," he says. "You. Go. Now."

I don't ask for clarification. I run out of the bar and into the cold night air.

As soon as I'm safely out of range, I start smiling. I fucking did it. Thank God. I can only imagine what would have happened if I'd stayed. I've heard that you get a permanent record that way, that you have to report it on a job application. But not me, I am home free. Golden. It's a second chance.

Just then someone jumps me from behind.

"What the—" But it's Jared.

"Dude," he says, "you are fucking awesome. Awesome!"

"You got off?"

"Totally. I said almost exactly what you said. Practically shit my pants, but I did it. And he fucking lets me go! I can't believe it! You're fucking brilliant!"

"Thanks." I do feel pretty amazing. Plus, in spite of everything, I can't help but think how cool it is that Jared is Ryan's best friend and he totally owes me, and I'm spending all this time with him. He'll tell Ryan how cool I am, and Ryan will see exactly how badly he screwed up, exactly what he's missing out on.

"We have to celebrate," Jared says.

"I don't think so. Haven't you had enough excitement for one night? Plus I have a paper to write."

"Well, from what I hear from Ryan, you're pretty much some kind of a genius."

I can't believe Ryan said this about me. Clearly, if I were just a two-night stand or whatever, he wouldn't have said this about me. If I was that to him, why even say anything about me? And how funny would it be to hang out with Jared now? When Jared comes home and Ryan asks where he's been, he'll have to say he's been with me. Ryan will have to be jealous.

"Celebrate how?"

"With drinks, of course."

"Of course. What was I thinking? Jared, it's almost three."

"How about your place?"

"Okay. You can come up. But not for long, got it?"

I wish I could be there when Jared gets home at five and tells Ryan about the night.

In the lobby, I sign Jared in. It's so weird to be here doing this when I know we won't hook up. The doors to all of the bedrooms are shut, so my roommates must be sleeping. I open up the refrigerator. All we have is a bottle of grain and some Crystal Light. From the looks of the kitchen table, people were here drinking shots earlier. Susan and Jane must have had company.

I put ice in two glasses and pour in a few inches of grain. Then I top them off with some grape Crystal Light and stir them with the handle of a used spoon from the counter.

"Crystal Light and grain?" Jared says. "You are unbelievable."

"It's delicious. You can't taste the grain at all." After two of them, I'm extremely buzzed again. So is Jared.

"Can I see your room?" he says.

I don't like where this is heading. The funny thing about school is, anything's possible when you're drunk and the night's been as surreal as tonight. Even though he was totally talking about Ryan to me just hours earlier, it's entirely possible, given the circumstances, that I could fool around with Jared now. But even in my semimuddled state, I know that would be a big mistake. I'm already embarrassed enough around Ryan. This would be humiliating. But Jared's eyes are brown-green and sparkly and he has huge dimples. Plus, he's got one of those bodies that makes a perfect V.

Still, I have to think beyond the moment. He walks into my room without waiting for me to answer. I follow him.

"Cool room," he says, looking at my Spinneybeck leather poster, rows and rows of colored leather baseballs on a black background. He starts reading from the wall. "'Home is where one starts from.' That's deep." Then he flops down on my bed and pats the space beside him.

"Yeah, right, Jared. That'll happen."

"C'mon. We're friends, right? Hang with me."

"All right. But move over."

"I am over!"

I take off my shoes and lie down beside him, as far away as I can be on a twin bed. Then the ceiling spins onto the floor. I inch closer to the side and drop my foot to the ground again.

"Bed spins?" Jared asks.

"Yeah."

"Me too." He can't reach the floor, though, because his side of the bed is pushed up against the wall. He braces one hand against the wall and reaches out with the other into the slim space between us. I hold his hand. "Ryan is a lucky guy," he says.

The room slows down. I like his hand around mine. The firmness of his grasp, the way the skin stretches across the long bones, the comfort of being small inside his bigger palm. "He doesn't know he's lucky," I say.

"He'll get it together, you'll see," says Jared, circling his fingers on the top of my hand.

"You know what the worst thing about tonight is?" I say.

"That we have to get new IDs somewhere. That'll be a bitch."

"No, not that. It's that I've been her for so many years, the girl in that ID. Not just carried her with me through all these phases of life, but actually been her. She was a part of me, know what I mean?"

"I think so."

"I feel so—I don't know. Lost without her. Like I'm missing a big piece of me." I take my foot off the floor and put my head on his chest. It's warm. His heart beats fast under my cheek. "What is an ID anyway? It's how you identify yourself to the world," I say.

Jared smoothes my hair, and we're quiet for a moment. "My grandfather died this year," he says softly. "My grandmother died a year ago. She had cancer. The grief probably killed my grandfather. They were really in love. They lived in Toronto, and we used to all fly up there for holidays. Man, it was so cold! You could feel it in your bones. We would make this great hot cider. But they were the only close relatives we had up there. Now that my grandfather's gone, we'll probably never go up there again. When we went up for the funeral, my mom looked at me and said, 'It's the end of an era.'"

"I'm sorry about your grandparents."

"Yeah. It's sad. And that's what this is, tonight. It's the end of an era."

Then we both fall asleep.

144

15
★
float like butterfly reprise

I wake up from confusing dreams with that feeling that something is very wrong. I look at the clock: 7:30 A.M. Jared's still here. "Shit!"

"What?" Jared says, rubbing his eyes. "What's up? Nothing happened, Beck. Don't worry. At least I don't think anything happened."

"Nothing happened. It's not that. It's my Art History paper. It's due in an hour and a half."

"Oh, man. Well, you can pretty much forget that one, right? Hand it in tomorrow." He rubs my shoulder and turns over to go back to sleep.

"But I don't do that. I don't hand stuff in late. It's just—I don't do that."

"So what are you gonna do?"

"Write the paper! I can do it. It's only a five-pager. Do you type?"

"Yeah, actually. But my contacts are like dried on."

"You owe me one, okay?"

"Yeah, I do," he says, sitting up reluctantly.

Jared sits down at my desk and boots up my Mac. "So, what are we writing about?"

"'Muhammad Ali' colon. 'Embracing Power and Weakness through an Image within a Nonimage.' Are you getting this?"

"I'm getting it, but I'm not getting it."

"Okay. Keep going. 'Is strength really what it seems? A work called *Float Like Butterfly* at the Philadelphia Museum of Art selects a complex subject and treats it simply. The piece consists of a large metal canvas on which the artist has painted the words *Float like butterfly. Sting like bee,* using what appear to be standard stencils. Drips of paint are visible at the points where the letters join. These drips are the only apparent evidence of the artist's hand.'"

"Whoa—whoa. Hold on a second," Jared says.

"'The spareness and size of the work capture the viewer's attention as does the power of the words themselves. The removal of the articles from the two featured sentences increases the strength of the message, as if the words are too important to require the niceties of language, as if they have broken free from the constraints of English. They read like a mantra, begging the viewer to speak them aloud over and over.'"

"This is good," Jared says, his fingers clicking away at the keyboard. "Ryan was right about you."

"Whatever. Don't write that. 'The use of stencils and metal and the scant references to the artist enhance the power of the words by forcing the viewer's attention there and by suggesting that the piece somehow—'"

"Slow down!"

"'—somehow goes beyond the notion of art as art. But the fact that the drips remain sets up a contrast, reminding us at once that beneath the almost mechanical elements there is a fragile hand at work, that beneath every strong surface exists a kind of weakness.

147

"'This contrast causes the viewer to question the impenetrability of the surface and fits the subtext of the work, namely that Muhammad Ali, the author of the original quoted material, was himself a man whose strength proved penetrable. Muhammad Ali has Parkinson's disease. His is a shaken legend. In that sense, the work celebrates not just strength as it may appear at first glance, but weakness too, as part of the underlying truth of any image or phrase or anything else to which we attach legendary status. The piece reminds us to question surfaces, and to make any examination a thorough and considered one, and in doing so, ultimately does make a statement about art itself, even while appearing to reject such a statement.'"

When the paper is done, Jared spell-checks it and prints it while I change my clothes and splash some water on my face. It feels strange to strap my book bag across my chest again. Like donning a foreign uniform I found in someone else's closet. Jared and I walk out together. In the elevator, he puts the pages in order and clips them for me.

"Thank you," I say when we're standing outside.

"No, thank you. You really saved me. It's been a memorable night."

"I gotta run." I kiss him on the cheek and he hugs me. My hair smells like last night's smoke.

"I'll see you around," he says.

I run down to class without stopping for breakfast. I know I must look terrible—I haven't even had time to put on my disguise.

I arrive, breathless, fifteen minutes late to recitation. I barely make it through the end of class. My eyes keep fluttering shut. When I go to hand in my paper, Ms. Slater, the TA, eyes me disapprovingly. Ms. Slater is one of those people I instantly dislike. She has a jutting chin that gives her a constant tough look and the kind of eyebrows that say, "Look, I'm not plucking my eyebrows!" She wears corduroy jumpers, Birkenstocks with rag wool socks, and a necklace with several crystals. Something in her carriage makes me suspect that she secretly lives in a town house in Society Hill and drives a BMW with a peace sticker on the fender.

"You were late," she says after class as I pack up my book bag.

That's a news flash. "I know. I'm sorry. I overslept."

"And I looked for you in lecture on Monday and didn't see you."

"It's a huge class!"

"So are you saying you were there?"

"I'm saying—I'm asking you to give me a break."

"Which somehow you deserve?"

"Ms. Slater, a lot of people skip classes. For no reason. A lot of people don't even sign up for 9 A.M. classes because they don't want to get out of bed. A lot of people hand things in late. I'm not one of those people, okay? I work hard. I just need a little break."

"No. It's not okay. Look, Rebecca, I'm sure I don't show it, because I don't like to play favorites, but you are the star of this section. I've told Professor Hartt about you. And I expect a little more from you than I expect from 'a lot of people.' I expect this to mean something to you."

You expect. They expect. But Number Six has fumbled the ball this time. And it actually feels pretty good. "The class does mean something to me, Ms. Slater. Look, I'm sorry if I don't always meet this standard that you've decided to hold me up to. But have some empathy, would you? There's a lot of stuff going on that has nothing to do with this class, or any class even." I push my hand through my hair. "And I'm still here doing the best I can do. Taking this seriously. But I can't be everybody's star all the time. Sometimes I get to sit in the back row. Sometimes I get to oversleep. I am tired."

149

"You say there's stuff going on. What stuff? Do you need to talk to somebody?"

"No. I don't. I need to get a break."

Students in the next class have started to filter into the room. I grab my things and push out the door.

Ms. Slater catches a handful of my sweatshirt in her hand. "Look, Rebecca, I think something is wrong. Can we talk about it?"

"Can't you just treat me like everyone else in this class? Can't you just let me sit back and screw up once in a while?"

Ms. Slater says nothing. Other students swirl around us, oblivious, gossiping about Halloween parties.

"No, of course not," I say. "From me, you have to expect perfection. I can't pause for one second, just check things out, see how the sky is looking. I have to keep going and going. I'm tired. If you don't mind, I'm going home to get a little rest. That is, if you're finished." I wrench my arm free and push out the door.

I know, without looking back, that Ms. Slater is still standing there at the front of the room staring at the space where I used to be.

I want to go home and sleep but it's almost eleven by the time Ms. Slater's done lecturing me, and I've got American Lit at one-thirty and I haven't done the work. We're reading *Moby Dick*. I walk up the steps to T-Square for some food to smuggle into the library. This is the architecture grad students' hangout. They all look so different and cool, with their dyed, gelled hair, big sunglasses, army pants, and black T-shirts, sitting around smoking Marlboro reds and drinking espresso. They seem so together, like a group with a plan. A few of them look at me as I walk in. I order a bagel with Monterey Jack cheese and a hot cider to go.

I walk into Rosengarten and find a carrel in the back where I can eat without anyone seeing. Then I rummage in my bag for my copy of *Moby Dick*. I don't get what's so great about this book. They're on the boat and everyone's talking about squeezing. It sounds vaguely homosexual, and I feel kind of left out. It just all seems so male and uninteresting. I wish we didn't have to read these things that are so far in the past when there's so much more exciting stuff going on in the present world that I really would like to read about, like about people in college, and drugs, and New York nightlife. But I'm stuck on a boat with a bunch of guys doing boring nautical crap in the middle of nowhere.

In class, Professor Birdy talks about how some critics say that all that stuff really is homosexual, how there's this undercurrent of sexual tension in all the squeezing, and reads these passages out loud in a kind of sexy voice, just to make the point really clear, with Ishmael and Queequeg and this quilt. At the end of class she tells everyone to pick up their papers. "Except for Rebecca Lowe," she says.

I feel my stomach drop. She's going to chew me out about my paper. She's a Whitman scholar and I've missed the point somehow or worse.

I raise my hand.

"You should see me," she says.

Of course. I make my way up to her desk. The TAs start calling out all of the other names and handing the papers back.

"Rebecca?" she asks, seeing me hovering there, miserable, scuffing one sneaker with the other.

"Yes. I'm Rebecca. That's me."

"Well, Rebecca, I just have to tell you personally that this is about the finest paper I've seen in my history of teaching this class."

"It is?" I feel myself blushing and look down again. "Thank you."

"No, I want to thank you. This is so original. So surprising. I was truly, truly impressed with your work. I've made a copy to keep, if you don't mind."

"No, I don't mind."

"Well, here you go. And I'll see you next class."

I take my paper from her. At the top it says, "A+—Brilliant."

"I've never given an A-plus before," she says, watching me look it over.

"Thank you." I slink out of the room as if she might take it back. People are swirling around me again, looking at their papers and being happy or not. I feel so completely other, out of place and removed and not belonging. Someone in the class who must have heard Ms. Birdy claps me on the back. "Good job," he says. I try to thank him but no words come out. I just stand there letting it soak in. It feels like it's the first paper I've done that's completely my own, even though it's not. I look at the A+ again, then fold the paper in half and jam it into the outside pocket of my book bag.

16

★

jouncing the limb

Maybe this is the answer then. Listening to my instincts. I saved Jared and me from trouble with the LCB. I was right that the paper was a good idea. Ryan said before that I played too many games rather than listening to my instincts, that I should have called him if I wanted to talk. Maybe that's the whole thing with him, that I'm supposed to be trusting my instincts more, doing what I want to do and not what every Miss Manners book on relationships says I should do. Then, before I can think it through, I go to the bookstore and buy a paperback copy of *Story of My Life*. With one of the bookstore pens, I scribble, "Ryan— Heard you were sick. Hope you're feeling better. Call me. Rebecca," on the inside. I walk across the Compass and past Wharton, stepping into the light that sprinkles through the trees so it washes over me. I leave the book at the Quad desk under his name. He was sick, after all. Maybe he just needs some comforting. Maybe he needs a break too.

When I get back to my room, I want to call my mother and rub my paper in her face, but she won't be home and doesn't take calls at work. She's a college counselor with her own consulting business. There's never a low season, though, because, according to my mother, you can always be doing something to make yourself a more appealing candidate.

I call my father instead. Barbara, his secretary, answers. "I'll put a note in front of him that it's you and we'll see if he'll take the call," she says. For a moment, I have a pang of worry that he won't pick up the phone and Barbara will have to tell me that my father just won't make time for me. I wait a couple of painful minutes. He takes the call.

"Hi, Rebecca."

"Hi, Dad. How are things going?"

"Very well thank you. A little crazy. Putting out a few fires. What's up?"

When he says that, when he sounds all rushed and distracted, I'm little again, sitting in our den trying to think of something worthy of telling him. Just a word, one word from him, that was everything. But he'd sit in that leather chair smoking his cigar, reading the paper, not even answering me. I used to say "Dad" over and over again, just waiting for some kind of an answer, trying to get his attention. Until my throat hurt. Until my voice got raspy. I used to hear myself saying his name in my sleep.

"I got an A-plus on my paper for Great American Writers. Will you tell Mom?"

"An A-plus? Wow. Is this that one on some kooky topic that she wanted you to redo?"

"It wasn't kooky. It was about Walt Whitman poetry and Jesse Jackson speeches. And my teacher said—"

"*Kooky* was her word and not mine. I think that's great news, honey. I'll let her know."

"I think she owes me an apology."

"Oh, come on. Because she said your idea was 'kooky'?"

"Because she is so unsupportive of me. She can't trust that I know what I'm doing."

"Well, I have to tell you," he says, chuckling, "you don't exactly act as if you know what you're doing."

"In what way, Dad? When I get all A's? When I never miss a class? When I never pass in an assignment late?"

"It just seems that every time we talk to you, you have some assignment that you're doing at the last minute and you're going out every night. Frankly, we're always amazed at how you seem to pull this stuff out of thin air."

"It's not out of thin air, Dad." I pace the room in circles. "When you say that, you act like every achievement of mine is like a magic act or a random stroke of luck. When really I'm smart and I work hard to get those results."

"We just wonder when it's going to end."

"When what's going to end?"

"You know, when some professor's going to call you on some of this stuff."

"So you're waiting for me to fail so that I can learn my lesson?"

"I didn't say that."

"Well, be prepared to wait a long time, 'cause it's not going to happen, Dad. I do things in my own way. But I do them well. I like that my life has some balance and festivity to it." I think of the lightness I felt, running from Smokes to freedom the night before. Now, making this argument to my father, I wonder if it's possible to put that upbeat feeling someplace, alongside the seriousness, the sadness even.

"It just bothers me this sense of entitlement you seem to have."

"Entitlement?" I feel like he's doused the candle I've just lit.

He takes a deep breath. "When I went to college, I studied every day. It meant something to me. But you think you're entitled to

156

go gallivanting around every night and just have everything fall into your lap."

"That's bullshit, Dad. I work hard too. Just because I time things differently or go out a lot doesn't mean I don't. Why is it any business of yours how I get my work done?"

"Your education is my business. I'm paying for it."

"Well, there you go, the great wallet speaks. The ultimate discussion-ender. Maybe I should transfer to Johns Hopkins and move home so you guys can keep a better eye on your investment."

"You're sounding pretty immature right now."

"You're patronizing me. You—reduce me to this. And you're right. It's awful. I hate the person I am in this conversation."

"I've got a lot of work to do," my father says.

"I've got a lot of reckless partying to do. Right? 'Cause that's all I do. Just don't forget to tell Mom thanks for all her help. Oh, and could you mention that my professor happens to be a famous Whitmanian scholar?" I hang up before he can respond.

"Fuck you!" I scream, banging the phone down. How do these phone calls get so supercharged and out of control? I only set out to have a moment of celebration. Maybe there was a gloating element there. But everything was fine until that "thin air" comment. And "entitlement." Why is it that, with one little phrase, he can pull just the right string, the one that makes me completely unravel?

I keep coming through and coming through and I just want one compliment, that's all, just one unadulterated "good job." I just want them to have a little faith in me. Or, better than that, I just want them to tell me one time that they love me unconditionally, that even if I don't come through, it's still okay. And I can't help feeling I'm entitled to that much. After the stuff that's happened, I feel like they owe me. I can make a catalog of debts, just by thinking back. I find myself doing just that sometimes, thinking back to the things they've done.

Just to make sure I don't forget. Somewhere in the middle of that catalog is the tonsil incident. I sit there by the phone, head in my hands, feeling myself go back there.

I had my tonsils out when I was almost fifteen. It hurt because I was older and because the tonsils themselves, the doctors told me at every checkup, were the size of golf balls. The surgery was tough—the nurse had trouble finding a vein for the IV, even as she stabbed and stabbed; the operation went longer than they expected; the tonsils broke apart as they removed them; the anesthesia took a long time to take.

My father was late picking me up. My parents were late a lot. I felt like I was always the last one waiting, at day care, after Sunday school, as if I were an annoyance or an afterthought. When he finally showed, I was starving and exhausted and the painkillers didn't seem to be having much of an effect either. On the way back to our house, I asked to stop at Cabot's for a milk shake. Sighing, he agreed. I think he was already annoyed that he, not my mother, had the job of driving me home. This veering from the plan—pulling off the highway where he usually maneuvered across the lanes so he could stay at eighty or higher all the way home, my having ice cream for dinner—annoyed him. He didn't offer to give me money for the shake.

I mustered up my energy, shuffled into Cabot's, and emerged with an extralarge raspberry sherbet freeze, which I was excited about; it seemed like something that would comfort me.

"All set," I said, struggling into the red leather seat.

But my dad just sat there. He'd turned off the engine.

"Let's go, Dad."

"I'm not driving with that open drink."

"But, Dad, it's not open. There's a lid."

"I'm just not going to, Rebecca. It'll spill everywhere."

158

"Dad, you have to listen to me, okay?" I say, holding my throat, my voice one step away from a whisper. Every word is abrasive. "I was in the hospital all day. I can barely keep my head up. I really need to lie down, take some of the Tylenols they gave me. I really want to go home. I'm so tired. I want my bed, Dad. Please."

"Look, I told you I'm not moving and I'm not moving." My father's voice was low, steady, utterly serious.

"Dad, do you have any idea how ridiculous you're being? It's not going to spill. Hello? Are you even listening to me? Jesus Christ, Dad. This car. You care more about this fucking midlife-crisis ridiculous car than about me. I'm not drinking the shake until you start moving."

"Rebecca, you had your tonsils removed. We're not talking about major surgery here. I'm a little surprised at how you're overreacting to this."

"What? Don't you think it's overreacting to love a car more han—"

"Don't be so dramatic." I heard a laugh at the edge of his voice.

I wanted to say something, but the combination of my already sore throat and that about-to-cry tightening made me unable to muster a word.

My father stared out the window.

We sat there in silence, neither making a move, for a really long time. Finally my father took off, intentionally jerking the car as he pulled away from the curb and at every stop sign. The straw jammed against my lips and against the roof of my mouth, but I said nothing. By the time we got home I could feel a film of sweat in my bangs. I got out of the car and slammed the door. I started to walk around the rear of the car to our front steps. And then my father, maneuvering the car into the narrow space in the garage, backed it up just slightly, without looking behind him.

"Jesus!" I screamed. He could have hit me. Time seemed to freeze, like in *A Separate Peace,* that line: *And then I jounced the limb.*

Later, my mother said supper was ruined because we were so late. My father said he didn't even come close to hitting me. But it's the fact that he didn't even look back that hurt. I wished momentarily that he'd revved the engine and really gunned it, rolling right over me. Then maybe he'd have felt bad.

I haven't moved from the floor; my hand is still inches from the phone. I think about how much I wanted to go home from the hospital that day, how much I wanted my parents to comfort me and take care of me. I try to remember a time when that happened, when my parents made me feel like I didn't have to worry, like everything would be okay. I've always thought that I'd earn that from them eventually, that there'd be this breakthrough moment, but I'm starting to come to terms with the fact the moment I've been waiting for isn't going to come. Nothing I do will ever be good enough. In their minds, I'll always be something short of what I could be. There will always be work to do.

It seems like a major feat of strength to lift myself from the floor, and as soon as I'm standing, I flop onto the bed. I know that I need to sleep now. First of all, I'm exhausted from the night before. And second, the argument with my father has made me really want to go out and go crazy tonight, so I need to rest up. But I'm still up too high on the adrenaline from the LCB bust and the A+ and the fight with Ms. Slater, and leaving the book for Ryan and now this. Just as I suspect, when I lie down, my eyes won't stop flickering.

I rummage around in my box of tapes until I find my old sleep tape. My mother bought it for me when I was little. I went through this period of terrible nightmares when I was eight. I would dream that bad guys were watching me all the time on hundreds of little TVs. Or that they were chasing me down a river in a speedboat and I had only my kickboard. I started to have trouble sleeping. So my baby-sitter, and sometimes, I think now, even my mom, would come in and put in the tape, which was the sound of waves lapping and rolling onto a beach. I remember my mom clicking the tape into place one night, leaning over to rub my back, whispering that she'd stay with me until I fell asleep.

I haven't heard the tape since I left home. Hearing it now doesn't make me fall asleep, though. I remember my mother's hand patting me on the back so softly and with so much kindness. Hoping that she wouldn't leave until I was safe. And now I find comfort in a million other places, or try to. And every interaction I have with my parents seems only to shake the comfort out of me, like ripping off a blanket I've laid across myself, leaving me totally exposed. I lie there, listening to the crashing waves and not sleeping, until the tape clicks and stops.

17

★

obituary

I can tell that Jane and Susan are buzzed by their voices and the way their keys jingle around the lock, missing the keyhole. They throw their books on the floor and run into my room. They climb all around me and blow gin-laced breath in my ears when they hug me hello. "Where were you guys?" I ask.

"Getladium," they giggle in near unison. This is our slang for the Palladium.

"In the middle of the day?"

"We were walking home from field hockey practice and a bunch of Sigma Chi guys were sitting outside."

"But it's freezing!"

"Not really," Susan says.

"It's sunny there," says Jane.

"They dragged us over," says Susan.

I'm sure.

"Scott Childs was there, by the way. He asked about you."

I roll my eyes.

"And you'll never guess who else was there!" Jane says.

"Who?"

"Your freshman."

I am instantly aware of my heartbeat. "He's not my freshman. I'm not even into him at all. There's just chemistry. It's not like I'm interested in having some kind of thing with him."

"Even if he wanted to?"

"Fuck you, Jane," I say.

I'm dying to ask what he was doing, who he was with. But I can't now.

"Beck, my God, why are you so touchy?" Susan says.

"I'm not in the mood for this," I say.

Susan and Jane look at each other. "Fine," Susan says. The two of them walk out of the room.

Then the phone rings. It's Phoebe.

"What happened to you last night?" I ask.

"You mean when I was talking to Chevs? Nothing. Same old, same old. It just—I don't know—touched a nerve. He still wants to be friends. I still don't think I can be. It just freaked me out seeing him there. We used to go there together, as a couple. I don't know."

"I'm sorry. That must be so hard."

"Yeah. I just got so upset I really had to leave. He walked me home. We looked for you but I couldn't find you."

"I got busted."

"Busted? No way? You mean the LCB showed up?"

"Yeah. You didn't hear?"

"No. I've been sleeping all day. What happened to you?"

"Nothing. I got out of it. But they got my ID."

"That sucks. But it's a good thing they let you go. I heard you get a record and have to take AA classes with a bunch of slimeballs."

"Maybe it would have been good for me."

"Are you serious?" she asks.

"No. I don't think so. Should I be?"

"I don't know."

Then we're quiet for almost too long.

"What are you doing tonight?" Phoebe says finally.

"I don't know. Feeling sorry for myself."

"Well, this really cute guy in my Religious Studies class gave me invites to the Pi Omega 'Lei Me' party. Do you want to go?"

Under normal circumstances, there's no way I'd go. I've never liked the Pi Omega brothers. Jane and Susan call them the POBBs—Pissed-Off Bar Mitzvah Boys. But what the hell. I'm happy to have a plan. And I feel like dancing.

"Who in Pi-O is really cute, Phoebe?"

"Oh, c'mon. Jake Levine. He's a senior."

"And he's taking Religious Studies?"

"He's premed!" Phoebe says.

"And he's over five feet tall?"

"You sound like Susan."

"Okay, okay. I'll go," I say.

"Okay. You have to dress tropically."

"Tropically? In November?"

"It's a Hawaiian theme," Phoebe says.

"I'll go, but I am not dressing tropically."

"I'll come over before. We'll put something together."

"Fine. We have to drink first," I say.

"I'll be over at ten-thirty."

"So do you really think I have some kind of problem?" I ask. "With drinking?"

"I don't know. I guess we all do. I think it's a college thing."

"Yeah. I think so too. It's not like it's interfering with my life, right?"

"Is it?" Phoebe says.

"What was the deal with Ridge Slocum, anyway?"

Ridge Slocum is this freshman in Sigma Chi who put himself into detox after hell week. Now he doesn't drink at all, carries around a liter of diet Coke at parties.

"I think he was drinking like first thing in the morning. Kept a bottle of JD under his bed or something."

"So that's totally different," I say.

"I think so."

"I'll see you tonight."

There's a knock at my door. It's Susan and Jane again. They're still giggly. "Are you in a better mood now?" Jane asks.

"Marginally," I say.

"Can we come back in?"

"Okay."

They climb back onto my bed. Susan puts my stuffed moose on her head. "How do I look?"

Then Jane puts my giant bear on her head and giggles.

I stick my head back under the covers.

"Oh, come on," Susan says. "What's up? Did you hear there was an LCB bust at Smokes last night?"

"Yeah, I heard. I got busted!"

"No way!" Jane says.

"I didn't see you," says Susan. "A bunch of us ran out the back door downstairs and through the tanning salon into the alley. Fleet McCauley ran into the kitchen, put on an apron, and started cleaning the grill. You really got busted?"

"Sort of. They took away my ID, but I said I wasn't drinking so they let me go."

"No way!" Susan says.

"Were you so scared?" Jane asks.

"Yeah, I was pretty scared. And now I have no ID."

"We'll get you another one," Susan says. "I think one of the seniors in Tabard has an extra passport."

"That would be great." But somehow it wouldn't be the same. I miss being Elspeth.

"No wonder you're so bummed."

"I also slept with the freshman." As soon as I say it, I know it's a mistake.

"You what?" says Susan.

"Yeah. I am no longer a card-carrying member of the V club." Both Susan and Jane are virgins. We've always made fun of how we're probably some of the last remaining virgins on campus. It's not so funny now, though. Because, when I say it, I know that it's real, that I'm no longer on the same plane, that I've crossed over into something else. Into Outsiderville. Where everything's blurry all of the time.

"So what's going to happen now?" Jane says.

Susan gives her a shut-up shove.

"Nothing's going to happen now, Jane. What do you think, we're going to ride off into the sunset together? It's just like any other thing you do."

"But it was your first time!" Jane says.

"So what. It's just like any other first time. It happens and then it's over. That's all."

"Is he not calling?" Jane asks. Susan glares at her.

"Do you hear the phone ringing, Jane?" I say. "I don't know if he'll call. I don't know what's going to happen next."

"When did it happen?" asks Susan.

"A few days ago."

"And you're telling us now?"

"We haven't really seen that much of each other, you guys."

"But Phoebe knows," Susan says.

"Phoebe knows," I say.

"You could have told me at Smokes."

"Yeah, Susan, I could have. But I just wasn't ready to, I guess."

"Do you need anything?" Susan asks. "Are you okay?"

"You used something, right?" says Jane.

"Of course I used something. I'm not an idiot. I'm fine. I don't need anything."

"Does this have to do with the football game? Did you sleep with him because of what was going on at the football game?" Susan asks.

"What was going on at the football game?" chirps Jane.

"I don't know. I don't know, you guys. Look, I need to get some rest. I pulled an all-nighter and Phoebe and I are going to the Lei Me party."

"With the POBBs? Why? Are you craving short men in loafers? Come out to Palladium with us. It'll be much more fun. Fleet is bartending. And we're going to FIJI after."

"No thanks. I want to dance. Maybe I'll meet up with you at FIJI though."

"Okay," Susan says. "Should I shut the curtains?"

Jane turns out the light and closes the door. I hug my knees to my chest and try to sleep.

I wake up at nine, feeling like I don't know where I am, even in my own room. It's like the morning at Trey's. I need to look around and calm myself, remind myself that I am home.

I have to read for my Holocaust Lit class, so I brush my teeth, take my book, and go up to the rooftop lounge in my sock feet. I can see everything from the giant windows: the red sculpture we call the Dueling Tampons, the president's mansion, the row houses of West

Philadelphia. No one else is here. I press my hands on the glass and feel my stomach sink. Then I make myself lean forward until my forehead touches, until I can feel myself falling. I imagine what would happen if the glass broke, where my body would finally stick, how mangled it would be, what the obituary would say: "Straight A's, so much promise. Always so upbeat. She used to sing in the shower. A good kid." "She was going to go to law school," my father would say, "and follow in a long tradition of Ivy League–educated lawyers in our family." Or maybe they'd interview Susan: "She suddenly got weird, after Number Six fumbled the ball. It was like that touched something off in her. She wasn't the Beck we used to know anymore." But the window holds.

I climb into one of the big, seventies-style couches. I finish the reading in an hour. It's the last part of *Survival in Auschwitz*. I don't actually think about it, though, I just get through it. Phoebe will be here soon and I need to get ready to go out.

The fried, sweet smell of General Gau's chicken hits me in the nostrils the second I walk back into our place. Susan, Jane, and Maggie are all sitting around the table. Jane has her knees up and picks at the crispy coating on a piece of chicken with a folded hand, like a small bird. "Hey, Beck," Maggie says.

"Hey."

"Where'd you go?" asks Susan.

"To read."

"Want some?" Maggie asks, pushing a carton of fried rice in my direction.

"No thanks. I'm not hungry."

"When was the last time you ate?" asks Susan.

I try to think. I can't remember, though. I know I've eaten since, but the french fries with the homeless guy are the last food I remember clearly. "Why?"

"You have to eat."

"What are you, my mother? I know when I need to eat."

"Relax," Susan says. "Don't take this out on us, Beck."

"Don't take what out on you?"

Susan looks at Maggie and Jane across the table.

"Leave me out of this," Maggie says. "I don't even know what's going on."

"Nothing is going on," I say.

"Yeah, it is," says Susan.

Jane seems to study the baby-pink polish on her fingernails. "You are freaking out, Beck," she says finally, her voice apologetic, barely audible.

"I think you should talk to somebody," Susan says. "You are not even close to the girl you were, like less than a week ago."

"How do you know, Susan? You don't even know me. We take a few classes together, go to some parties together, drink some shots together. What does that even mean? You don't know what girl I was or what girl I am."

"Do you?" Susan asks.

18

★

photograph

Phoebe knocks on the door. She's wearing jeans, sandals, and an open Hawaiian shirt with a man's ribbed tank top under it. She looks good. "Excuse us," I say, and shuttle her back to my room.

"What's going on?" Phoebe asks. "The tension's so thick in here I could cut it with a knife."

"Do you think I'm freaking out?"

Phoebe pauses and seems to choose her words carefully. "I think you're going through something that's really hard. But good. You're questioning yourself and you've been through some stuff that's made you have to rethink some things."

"I am completely obsessed with Ryan. I just—I just keep wanting to make things right with him. Or get some closure or something."

"I don't think it's closure you really want."

"It would be better than this," I say.

"Maybe."

"Oh, God, Phoebe. It's so hard. I don't know why it hurts so much. I don't even know him." I start to cry. "I want a boyfriend."

"Do you? If that's really all you wanted, then why not Scott Childs? Or Trey?"

"So what are you saying, that I have some real feelings for Ryan? I've barely even talked to him. I don't even know how he takes his coffee."

"I don't know that it's about having real feelings or not. It's more like you want to save him."

"What are you talking about?"

"You want to feel like here's this kind of bad, fucked-up guy, and you can come along with all your love and everything else and break through to him, finally."

"Where do you get that?" I ask, thinking already that there's some truth to it.

"I kind of felt that way with Chevs, that maybe I could make him turn good. Sometimes I still do."

"You do?"

"Of course. It's only natural."

"And then what? What do you want after this big break-through?"

"You want to have all these intense feelings of love that he's never had for anyone else, because no one else could ever get through to him. You want to be Ryan's one savior."

"Say that's really what it is, that I want to save him. What's the point? What happens then?"

"First of all, there's no then, because it's never going to happen. Which of course you know. But I think the thing is, that in exchange for saving him, you think he's going to save you back."

"I am such a moron," I say.

"We all are. It's not like you're the only one."

"I gave him a book."

"What?" Phoebe asks.

175

"I went to the bookstore and bought a copy of *The Story of My Life* and left it for him at the Quad desk."

"And did he call?"

"Nope. Can you believe that? He didn't even call to thank me. I left it right after my one-thirty recitation."

"Maybe he's still sick," Phoebe says.

"I wish. Susan and Jane saw him at the Palladium this afternoon."

"You know what, though, Beck? This thing started happening before things with Ryan got so upsetting. I mean, you were bummed out about things before. It was the call from your mother, and the game, and a whole bunch of other things probably, coming together."

"I guess."

"You've heard the expression *sophomore slump,* right? It happens to a lot of people. Don't give Ryan so much credit. It's like you said, you hardly even know him. If you're a little obsessed with him, it's probably not really even because of him but because of all these other things."

"Maybe."

"You should get in the shower. It's after ten."

By the time I get out of the shower, Phoebe has assembled an outfit for me: jeans, flip-flops, a white T-shirt and a white man's oxford. I put it on and she ties the shirt at my waist and puts a bottle of Bain de Soleil in the pocket. Then she mixes some brown blush with some moisturizer and starts "tanning" my face.

"Put on your sunglasses," she says. "Hey, where'd you get this? It's great?"

It's a tan hat of chino material with a grosgrain band of maroon and one of navy, hanging on a peg inside my closet door. "It was my father's when he was my age." I hadn't even looked at it since I'd hung it on that peg when I got here. I used to wear it all the time in high school, though. It was kind of a trademark. It's the hat my father's wearing in the photograph on my wall, standing in front of his Thunderbird. He looks jaunty and upbeat, but somehow a little scared too.

I want to go back and know him then. Before I was born. Before all of our fights and his stress about the job. He was scared too. We could have helped each other. I want to climb into that picture, back when everything seemed so hopeful, back before therapy and anxiety, and mortgages and arguments and adolescence and drawer-slamming and SATs. I want to make all those layers of bad stuff disappear. I want to go back and make us both different people, to unsay some of the hurtful things we've said to each other, to undo some of the mean things we've done. Maybe I could call more. Maybe I could just tell him I love him, even if he might not say it back.

I want to give him more chances.

"Phoebe, do I have time to call my dad?"

My father answers on the first ring.

"Hi, Dad. How are you doing?"

"Oh, are you talking to me now?" he asks.

I had almost forgotten how roughly we'd ended our last conversation. "Yeah. I'm wearing your hat."

"What hat?"

"The chino one with the blue and maroon ribbon around it."

"My parents bought me that at Brooks Brothers just before I went away to school."

I pull the phone away so he won't hear that I'm getting choked up.

"Dad, were you scared?"

"What? What are you talking about?"

"In that picture. When you're about to go to school. Were you scared at all?"

"I don't remember," he says.

"How can you not remember?"

"I don't think I was scared. I was excited to be getting away from home."

"Why?"

"You know what my parents are like, Rebecca. They put a lot of pressure on us. Telling us we had to be number one. I was going away to school and I was getting away from all of that. Getting out from under their thumb."

"And they had wanted you to go to Harvard."

"Right. And I was wait-listed."

"So you were about to go away and get away from them, but not really, because you were still expected to perform. And on top of that you had already disappointed them, kind of, because they had wanted you to go to Harvard. Wasn't that a little scary?"

"I guess it was."

"You look so young in the picture, Dad."

"I was young. And I was expected to be tough and to handle everything myself. It wasn't like with you and me, where we drove you down to school and helped you take care of your housing and all that. My parents just gave us one lump sum of money and we had to make it last the whole four years. That was all you got. And you had to find your housing and have a budget. You're lucky, because your mother and I don't believe in burdening you with all that stuff. You know how much we love you. With my parents, you never even talked about love. It was all very businesslike. They never told me they were proud of me."

"But, Dad, are you really so different from them? Even though we say 'I love you'? How am I supposed to know that you love me, from the things you do? Like only calling to ask about my grades, like telling me I missed you too much at camp?"

"At camp? I don't even know what you're talking about."

"Yes, you do, Dad. It's okay to say it."

"That was a long, long time ago, Rebecca. You've always melo-dramatized that whole thing."

"See, Dad! That's exactly what I mean. Melodrama? Those were my feelings, and they were real to me."

"Why is it that you only remember the bad things? We had a lot of good times together too, you know."

"Like when, Dad? Mom says that when I was little, if my diaper needed to be changed, you'd make a face and hand me back to her."

"Do you remember that time we went to Boston?"

"We never went to Boston. What are you talking about?"

"We did. You were about five years old. I had some business there, and your mother had parents' day at the school where she was teaching then, so I took you with me."

"No, Dad, I don't remember."

"I took you to Fenway Park to see a Red Sox game. You loved it. We got bleacher seats the day of the game. Everyone there went nuts for you. You were the happiest kid."

"Was it a good game?"

"Oh, yeah. Yankees. A close one too. Everyone was going crazy, yelling and screaming. So you got a little scared. I felt your lit-tle hand reach out for mine."

"So what did you do?"

"What do you mean, what did I do?"

"Did you hold my hand?"

"Of course I did. I held it the whole game. Except when I was shelling your peanuts. You never knew that? That's when you first started to love baseball. Remember, someone gave you that Carl Yastrzemski autograph; I think that was a few years later. Then in seventh grade you read *Great Gatsby* and you became completely obsessed with the Black Sox scandal."

Those other parts I remember clearly. But not Fenway. The closest I can get to remembering is our hands, my father's and mine. I remember, but without any context, sliding my hand into the curve of his, feeling safe.

"Maybe my standards are high, but I've always been proud of you," my father says. "I can admit that I'm not perfect. You're right. But I'm what you've got. You may not like it, but you only have one father. I love you, and I would never want any other daughter."

I can't believe what he's just said. I know I'll think of it over and over. *I've always been proud of you. I would never want any other daughter.* But I'll never again be right there, in that moment, when my father actually tells me that I'm good enough. If I had known it was coming, I would have done everything in my power to make it last.

"Dad, I wish I could have known you when that picture was taken. When you were a little scared. Your face looked so different; nothing had been written on it yet. I wish I could have just had one conversation with you."

"That was a long time ago," he says.

"I know."

19

★

fubar

"Are you okay?" Phoebe asks when I come back out into the living room.

I nod, then stand there without moving while my eyes well up with tears.

Phoebe gets up. "Bad stuff with your father?"

I shake my head. "Not bad. Just hard. Why does it have to be like that?"

She hugs me and pats my back. "Because if it wasn't, we'd all live at home forever."

I laugh. "Can you keep reminding me of that?" I say, mixing a cocktail at the sink and dabbing at my eyes with a dishrag.

"C'mon, let's go."

"Okay. One more sip."

The yard of the Pi-O house is decorated with a huge banner that says "Lei Me, Baby" and a bunch of plastic leis. Inside, they're blasting "She Drives Me Crazy" by the Fine Young Cannibals.

There's this huge, empty floor, but people are just bumping around on the edges, just like at a bad bar mitzvah.

"I don't know how long I can handle this," I say.

"There's Jake Levine!"

Phoebe's right; he is good-looking. Medium height, broad shoulders. His outfit is completely un-Hawaiian—jeans, gray V-neck sweater, white T-shirt, bucks. It's almost anti-Hawaiian, except someone has thrown a plastic lei over his head—but he's wearing it backward, so the front part is short and it dangles down his back. He's got the kind of shaded features that make him seem to get handsomer the more you look. "Hey," he says, tapping Phoebe on the shoulder. "I'm glad you came. Do you want to dance?"

Phoebe looks at me.

"Go ahead," I say.

I watch them from the side of the room for a while. Jake is a good dancer. He pushes his shoulders forward in a way that makes him seem extremely relaxed.

Phoebe gestures for me to come out onto the dance floor, but I'd feel like a loser, standing there dancing with the two of them. But then Jake leaves and I finish my drink in one sip and dance my way over to Phoebe. "So, what's happening?" I say.

"He just finished telling me how psyched he is to have a 'friend' in his Religious Studies class, since he could really use some help studying for the final. Can you believe that?"

"Let's see. I gave someone a gift and got no form of acknowledgment whatsoever. So, yeah, I can believe that."

"And what kind of moron needs help with Religious Studies as a senior?" Phoebe asks.

I shrug and keep dancing.

"I know, I know," she says, "you told me so. I just can't believe that he's going to be a doctor. That's a scary thing."

"We don't actually know that he'll make it through med school."

Phoebe follows my glance across the room. Jake is dancing with a skinny sophomore in SDT with size-D boobs on a size-four body. She looks over his head for something better and shakes her permed, streaked hair. "My Prerogative" by Bobby Brown comes on. The SDT gets all excited and wiggles her tiny hips. Jake gives them his undivided attention.

"Do you want to go?" I ask.

"No way. We're already here, and the drinks are free. Actually, this is good for my ego. It makes me feel tall."

Phoebe and I, at about five feet six inches each, are taller than most people in the room. "In that case," I say, "we'll be needing more punch." We walk over to the table labeled FUBAR (fucked up beyond all recognition) and ladle out several cups of the red punch for each of us. We each down all but one while we're standing at the table. Then we go back out on the dance floor. They're playing "I Wanna Have Some Fun" by Samantha Fox. We know all the words. We start screaming. People clear the space directly around us. We wave our hands over our heads.

We dance until it's three and everyone has cleared out. I have toilet paper on the bottom of my shoe. "I'm starving," I say.

"Wawa?" Phoebe asks.

We leave the house and no one says good-bye. We cross over the Walk to Spruce Street. Wawa is lit up and crowded. People prowl the aisles with cans of Pringles stuffed under their arms. I open the freezer door and pick out a pint of Chunky Monkey. We find a table by the window. Phoebe hands me a spork and a napkin.

"This could almost qualify as an aerobic activity," she says, digging for chocolate chunks and then handing the pint to me.

"Phoebe, remember when I had to go home that time last year?"

"When your grandfather was sick?"

"Yeah. Only he wasn't sick."

"What do you mean?"

"It was my uncle. He died. I went home for the funeral."

"Which uncle? Why didn't you tell me?"

"My uncle Dan."

"Your favorite uncle? The one who went to Penn? But he was younger than your father."

"Yeah. It was a drug overdose. He died from a drug overdose."

"What? Are you serious?"

"He was addicted to cocaine. And I don't even know what else he was doing."

"But I thought he had it made. Wasn't he working at some big law firm?"

"He didn't want to be, though. He wanted to be a photographer. He tried, after law school, but it never panned out. That's when he joined the firm. It was the eighties and everyone was doing drugs, I guess. He just never stopped."

"I'm so sorry."

"I never even talk about it with my father. It's like this thing that we don't talk about it. Even when it was happening. He was in a coma for a while and we always went to visit him separately. I went every day over Christmas vacation. I told him about all the cool stuff I was doing at Penn, taking that creative-writing class and everything. I begged him to snap out of it."

Phoebe puts her hand on my forearm. "That's so sad."

"The thing is, he was a kid who went to Penn. Just like me. And I can't help wondering, what made him crack? What made him fall apart? Because something must have made it all seem like it was too much."

"That's not you, though, Beck. You were like him, but that's not you. You aren't falling apart. You are the one who keeps everyone else together."

"But maybe he was too. Maybe he just got tired. Fumbled the ball."

"Listen to me," Phoebe says. "You've got to get ahold of yourself. You are not him. You're doing just fine. It's okay to drop the ball. You're still going to be all right."

Then I look down and see, in the harsh, convenience-store light, that I'm covered with FUBAR. My shirt is stained—sticky and red. So is Phoebe's. I start to laugh. Phoebe does too. How could we have not noticed before?

A skinny, red-haired guy walks by our table and then stops. "I hear the Pi-Os always piss in the FUBAR," he says.

20
★
we are here

We're still sitting at the table in Wawa, laughing and buzzed, when Jake Levine walks in. I kick Phoebe under the table. He's alone. He walks over to us.

"So this is where you ran off to," he says.

"You looked busy," Phoebe says.

Jake blushes. It suits him. "Yeah. Jen."

"Your girlfriend?" Phoebe asks over her shoulder as she fills a cup with ice at the deli counter.

"We've been on and off for a while. I guess we're off right now. She's not exactly my type, know what I mean?"

"She seemed like your type to me," I say.

Jake smiles. "Let's put it this way: she's a nice girl, but she's not splitting any atoms."

"That's nice, Jake," Phoebe says.

"You're right. You're right. I shouldn't bad-mouth her."

He looks at me with an ashamed expression that I appreciate.

Phoebe rolls her eyes and chews on her ice cubes.

"They say that's a sign of sexual frustration," Jake says.

Phoebe chucks a cube at Jake and he ducks. It cracks against the window.

"Oh, shit!" I touch my head. I don't have my hat on anymore. It's not on the table, either. "My dad's hat!"

"It's not here?" Phoebe asks, looking under the table.

I shake my head. Phoebe walks back to the freezer where we picked out the ice cream.

"You weren't wearing a hat at the party," Jake says.

He's looked so closely at me. It makes me feel good, more than it maybe should. He's seen me. "I wasn't?"

"You were dancing with Phoebe and your hair was swinging around." I feel my face warm. I raise my eyes a little to meet his. He's looking right at me.

"It's not here," Phoebe says.

"Maybe it's back at the house somewhere," Jake says.

"I just—it has sentimental value," I say. I think about when my father gave me that hat. We must have had a connection then; he was handing me the torch, all of his wishes for me, that I would go on and become something, maybe something he could never become. And now I've proven him right, proven my carelessness after he's trusted me.

"I understand," Jake says. "If you want, we can go back and look for it."

I look at my watch. It's almost four. My Holocaust Lit class starts at nine. I'll be exhausted now, no matter what I do.

"You don't mind?" I ask.

"No problem," Jake says. "Phoebe, we'll walk you home on the way."

So I go with him.

I don't think I'm still drunk, but my legs teeter and bang against the chair when I stand up. I nearly fall.

"Whoa—you all right?" Jake asks, holding my arm and putting a hand at the small of my back.

Phoebe watches us carefully.

"I'm fine," I say.

I steel myself for the coatless walk. We slip into the still black morning; our breath smokes the air. I walk carefully, placing my feet by the lines on the sidewalk. When we get to Phoebe's, I give her a big hug. "Bye, sweetie," I say. "Talk to you tomorrow."

"Take care of her," Phoebe says to Jake over my shoulder. "Do you want me to go too?" she whispers.

"I'm okay. It's late," I whisper back. "But is this okay with you?"

"Your walking home with Jake? My God, after tonight? He could fall in the Schuykill River and it would be okay with me. Just be careful."

"Don't worry."

"Ready?" Jake asks, taking a step toward me. We wave good-bye and head back toward Pi-O. He pulls off his scarf and wraps it around me. "You must be freezing," he says. The scarf is still warm from his neck. It smells like expensive aftershave. He turns up his shirt collar.

"Thanks," I say.

"You still cold?"

"A little. I'm okay."

"Here." He takes a slender flask from the pocket of his pants, unscrews the top, and hands it to me.

It's Jack. I take a sip, offer it back, and when he shakes his head, I have some more. There's a long pause. The street noises all sound loud against it, doors slamming, people yelling about tacos. "So do you guys really piss in the FUBAR?" I ask. I want to lighten the mood, but it doesn't work.

"Who told you that?" Jake sounds a little angry. But then we are here. He opens the heavy door and ushers me in. "Can I get you a drink?"

190

I don't want to be nervous; I'm just here to find my hat. A drink would take the edge off, make this seem more normal than it does now that Phoebe is gone. "Okay." I forget to tell him what I like.

"So," he says, bringing two glasses into the now deserted, littered living room, "where were you at the party?"

"I was dancing." I sip on what tastes vaguely like a vodka tonic. I feel something reignite.

"Just dancing in here?"

"I'm not sure."

He walks to the back of the room where the couches have been pushed against the wall. He sticks his hand underneath the cushions but doesn't find anything. "C'mon," he says, heading for the stairs.

"Upstairs?" His back, through the thin T-shirt, is beautiful. I watch the muscles move like boat blades. I don't think I was upstairs. "But—"

"Maybe one of the guys thought it was his. It was a man's hat, right?"

This makes sense enough to me. I look at my watch. The hands blur across the dial. Everything I try to touch feels like it's coated in sugar crystals and can't quite be reached. It's okay though, plenty of time to be kissed before my Holocaust Lit class. *He should bring the hat downstairs for me.* I try to clear my head a little, to remember what Phoebe said about Jake, if she still likes him. I don't think so, but I can't quite remember the conversation we whispered on the walk. "Be careful," I think she said. I want to be kissed.

"Wait," he says, bounding back down the stairs, which I've just started to climb tentatively, grasping the railing. He grabs my half-empty glass. "I'll get you a refill." In seconds he's back.

My glass is so full I have to take a big sip from the top right away. "What is this?"

"Grain and something. Hi-C. We ran out of tonic." He's back on

191

the stairs again, climbing faster than me, talking over his shoulder. When I say nothing, he turns and sees how I'm struggling a little. I'm working out how to hold both my drink and the banister. He reaches a hand behind him. I take it. The fingers are strong and warm. I tingle through the alcohol numbness.

In the hall at the top of the stairs, I see a cardboard box leaning against the wall. In marker on the side it says "Lost and found—parties." It's right there on top—my father's hat. Stained a little with FUBAR but otherwise unharmed. I see the black-and-white photograph in my mind's eye. My father, when he was young like me.

"That's it!" I feel so happy. I put my drink down in the middle of the hall, rush to the hat, grab it, and put it on. "Oh, whew, this is so great, this is so—"

"You look great."

I'm concentrating on the hat and thinking how I should probably get back now, just forget the kissing and this tension, which maybe I only imagined anyway, and leave with my hat and finally get some rest, so I almost don't hear him, but I do. I look up at him and he's looking at me in a way I like, but it's almost too serious, and I get nervous again. For a second I think about Plaid Shirt and Sig Tau, how I made a little deal with God, how I vowed I'd never be in a fraternity house alone with a guy again—and here I am. I look at my feet, flex my toes. I feel a bit unsteady. I put the palm of my hand flat against the wall.

And in the spins of this deep buzz and how happy I am and how the whole night has become blurred somehow, like time isn't even moving forward, and nothing seems to have a beginning that I can point to, nothing seems real, it seems only natural that he's picking my drink up off the floor, holding his and mine in one hand, his fingers inside the rims of the cups, and then pulling my hand off the wall and lacing my fingers with his, kissing me, pressing our bodies together, pushing the door to his room open behind him with the flat of his shoe, walking us backward onto the bed, putting our drinks on the nightstand.

I fall down on top of him, but he turns me over, takes off my hat, and puts it on the nightstand too, pulls my hair to one side like a curtain, and kisses my neck there. I feel the snowballing start again, like I'm rolling down a hill too fast and getting dizzy, even though some things are good, like this, like the way his hands push my hair away. I've forgotten why I'm here. "Jake, wait."

"No, no, shhh." He presses his lips onto mine.

It's mean, I think, the way he's shushed me.

"Jake, I said wait." I pull his hands off my stomach, and out from under my T-shirt, and he lets me and rolls over so he's beside me now, but then he brings one hand to my arm and starts circling the skin there with the pads of two fingers.

"Okay," he says, smiling, "I'm waiting."

"Why are we doing this?"

Jake lifts my shirt a little, but not enough to see anything, and puts his hand on my rib cage. I suck in my breath. I think about how narrow my rib cage is. It must feel good to him. I wait for him to touch me more. He runs his fingers along the edge of my bra. My face gets hot. He nudges open my mouth with his and slides his tongue in gently, making little plunges and circles in my mouth. Then he reaches down with the other hand and starts unbuttoning my jeans.

"No, stop." I push his hand to the side. I can't let him do this. Especially not here. I know I'll regret it. What am I going to be, some frat-house slut who people point out at parties? I have to get in control. "Stop."

"Okay. Okay." He's short of breath.

I breathe again, feel my pulse slow a little. Then he starts again. His hands are on my shoulders, and then he's kissing me, holding my face in his hands like I've always wanted someone to do, like in movies. He's unhooking my bra and I let him. He slides it off with my shirt, pushes his own shirt up so we'll be touching. It feels good. This is all I'll do.

He's rubbing my shoulders, then running a finger down my cleavage. "You are so hot."

"Thanks." I feel embarrassed. Something about his words or his breathing makes this the same as when he shushed me before. I feel like he's yelling at me, the jolt and aggressiveness of this.

He plays with my hair and looks at me until I have to look away. I catch the hat on his nightstand in my line of vision and think about how pretty soon I'll take it and I'll be leaving.

Then he's reaching for my jeans again, and I've buttoned them back up, but he's not unbuttoning them this time, just reaching inside, and sighing when he touches me. It happens so fast and it seems like I can only react in my head; it takes me too long to say anything.

"Jake, stop, stop!" I say, catching up.

Only he keeps going, rubbing me and then rubbing himself against me.

"Jake!" I suddenly feel something sharp-edged crashing down around me. I feel myself pulling through the softness that was there before, sobering. "I said stop!" I fling his hand away and it bangs the side of the bed.

"Owww!" He sits up, rubbing his hands together.

"I'm sorry. But I said stop." I'm buttoning my jeans back up.

"Yes, yes, you did," he says. "I'm sorry."

"I should go. Will you walk me home?"

"Walk you home?"

"Yes, walk me home. Escort isn't running this late. I'm not going to walk by myself."

"We're right near the Walk."

"You asshole! I'd have to cross Walnut Street, first of all, only a few blocks away from where there was a shooting, what, a week ago? And no one will even be on the Walk."

"You're right. I'm sorry. I guess I just wanted you to stay." He reaches for the point of my chin with two fingers and pulls me toward him again. I like the way his eyes are light brown but the lashes are so dark. I like the olive color of his skin. I feel stupid for being scared before.

"I have to go."

"Okay. I'll walk you home. You're absolutely right about not going home alone. I'm an asshole."

"You're not an asshole."

"So does that mean I can kiss you one more time before we go?"

"Okay." I smile a little.

He leans forward slowly, making me wait. He puts his hand just on my chin, holding my face like before. Then he strokes the side of my cheek and grasps my whole face, his hands in my hair. It feels like the room has a pulse again. He kisses me, almost without tongue, just long and confident, and our chests are touching again, and I'm outlining the muscles on his back with my hands and letting him pull me horizontal again, even though I know I should stop him.

And suddenly I look down and he's pulled my pants open again. Even though he said he wouldn't.

"Hey!" I yell.

"Shh, c'mon. Don't be a tease."

"A tease? What are you talking about?"

"You're up in my room in the middle of the night. You were staring at me on the dance floor."

"What?"

"No, it's cool. I liked it. I'm just saying—"

"You're just saying what, exactly?"

"I'm just saying that you should relax a little, go with the flow."

"It's late. Will you please just walk me home?"

"I will. I promise. Okay? But let's not go yet." He reaches forward, tucks my hair behind each ear. "Here, let me rub your back."

I do. While I weigh my options, I turn my back to him, pressing my knees to my chest to cover myself. He rubs with the cool assurance of someone who knows he's good, just the way he kisses. I feel him pressing out some of the tension; my shoulders relax. Then I spot what's left of my drink on the nightstand. The ice has all melted and the bright cranberry color has faded to a watery pink. I start to count the beads of condensation. Then I reach out my arm, slide the glass off the table, take a long sip, finishing it.

"Your back is really nice," he says.

"Thanks."

"You could stay here if you wanted to. It's closer to your class. I don't mind."

"I have to get my books. I have to go home."

"So you really take this seriously. That's cool."

"Maxx is great. So, yeah, I take it seriously."

"I had him as a freshman. He never really liked me, though."

"How could that be possible?" I say it a little meanly, a little jokingly.

"Ha, ha." He pushes me a little, like a brother.

I turn to face him, push back, until we are wrestling. That's when I decide. I'm already in his room. It's just too hard to get out of this now. He'll be so much happier with me if I just go along and sleep with him. And it won't be such a big deal; it'll be over in five minutes. Then I can go home. I look at my watch. I can still get an hour of sleep before class starts.

So when the wrestling turns back into something else, I don't stop it. Not that I would have had much of a chance to. He unbuttons my pants and slides his finger in, all in one motion. I'm dry inside and I wish he'd just hurry up, get to the sex part and be done. "Do you have anything?"

"Yeah." His breath sounds strange, ragged like a cough after a long night of smoking, as he reaches back to the nightstand, fiddles with the drawer.

I draw up, hold my knees to my chest again, until the very last second, until he turns back and I know I'm supposed to look the way I looked before, all laid out for him, all ready.

He props up one arm, turns his back to me. I hear the wrapper crinkle. I think of my white bed in the high-rise. I see myself in my faded flannel nightie from junior high, holding my stuffed animals, sleeping with the shades drawn and a cup of chicken soup by the bed. He's pressing into me now. I wonder why it still hurts. My sheets are going to feel so cool and clean. There's a brown water stain on the ceiling, curved like a leaf. The tiles have little punctures. The molding around the edge of the room breaks in two places. In just a little while, I'll be home. I watch his shoulder blades working. His face doesn't look handsome anymore. I wish I could go back to when I was standing downstairs. And everything was kind of okay. I wonder if my roommates will be able to tell that I did this. Will they look at my face and know?

He shudders and he stops moving and I guess it's done, but I'm not sure. "Did you—"

"Yeah," he says, out of breath. He looks at me like I'm stupid or like I'm something he didn't think I was before. He lifts out of me, reaches for his drink on the nightstand, and gulps the rest. I watch his Adam's apple bob and wonder how long until I can get dressed.

"So—"

"Shhh. Just rest." He pats the space beside him.

And in literally seconds, he's asleep. This can't be happening. After all that, he's not going to walk me home? "Jake," I shake his arm. Nothing. I shake it harder. I pull so hard I think I might take the arm out of the socket. He doesn't stop snoring for a second.

I think about the bleak stretch of deserted Walnut Street between here and the Walk. I gather my clothes from the floor, hook my bra back on, slide on the stained T-shirt, thinking of the FUBAR, how happy we were, dancing, Phoebe and me. I don't know if I can finish this job of getting my clothes on and getting out of here. I stop, wipe my eyes with the sleeve of my shirt, inhale the cottony smell, steel myself to keep going. I put on my father's hat and negotiate the stairs in the dark.

The sky and the streets are gray. My steps echo across this emptiness. I want to laugh at the times I thought I was lonely before. I see a homeless man watching me head toward the street. My chest tightens. I remember this story my mother told me of this girl my age who was stabbed in the throat by a homeless man as she jiggled the keys in the lock of her Manhattan apartment. But when he walks by, he only smiles at me. I feel a piece of me slide away.

At the Walk, I see some of the rowers jogging to morning practice. One of them I kissed; he nods his head at me and checks to see if his teammates have seen. If I sat still for a minute and tried to remember all the kisses, could I? I'm not sure. They all seem the same. All the nights blurred and overlapping. All the next-day conversations: Phi Delt was so much fun. Zete was so much fun. Sigma Chi was so much fun.

I slide my ID through the turnstile and let go. I am home again.

21

★

in the compass

Inside, I go directly to the bathroom. I run a shower of only hot water and take off my clothes as fast as I can, avoiding the mirror. I lather and lather the soap, scrubbing at the door stamp on my hand with Jane's pumice stone. I emerge red as a newborn. The steam surrounds me, follows me into my room. I take out my book bag and pack for class: pens, highlighter, the Primo Levi book, my loose-leaf. It's hard to believe the stuff with Jake actually happened. The sky is such a different color now. But fragments keep coming back: concentrated breathing, a tone with an edge of anger, something being rubbed the wrong way.

I put on some cotton underwear, sweatpants, a T-shirt, a sweatshirt over that, and slide into bed. The sheets are cool as I'd hoped, only it took so long to get here. In half an hour I have to get ready for class. I lie on my back first, then fold my hands across my chest. Then I roll onto my side and curve my knees into a ball. I stay that way, thinking of all of the things I could have done differently, until my alarm goes off.

I almost forget that Susan and I both have classes across

campus this morning. We usually walk together. I look in the mirror. My face is the color of dirty walls. I take out my makeup bag. I want to look like someone else today or like someone I was before—wasn't it just a few days ago when I skittered to class early to pick up a copy of *34th Street,* busying myself reading the gossip column while I waited to see if Daniel Miller, the sometimes sexy class radical, would slide into the chair beside me, his long arm extending around my back? Maybe it was a week ago. The shadows under my eyes resist the ivory-colored makeup. I pull on tights, the first clothes I grab, everything black. The thing is, about last night, I can't think that it was rape. It wasn't rape. I said okay. So I could get it over with. So I could get home. There isn't anything wrong with that. A lot of people sleep with a lot of people.

At eight forty-five I knock on Susan's door.

"Uh-huh," she says through clenched teeth.

I open the door and find her standing on a chair in front of her closet, staring at four piles of brightly colored Benetton sweaters with a tube skirt on a hanger in her mouth. "Stand" by R.E.M. is playing on her box. I remember an interview with R.E.M. that I heard on the radio. They said that "Stand" was the stupidest song they ever wrote and they had no idea why so many people liked it. But everyone likes a good hook.

"You're not ready?" I say, surprised, even though Susan is never ready. Somehow I have forgotten all the usual details. I feel like I've been away somewhere, again.

"Almost," she says. "So, what happened at Pi-O last night? I never heard you come home."

"Nothing. We went to Wawa late night. The usual." I think about laughing with Phoebe while we ate the Chunky Monkey ice cream. I could have just gone home after that. "You're not blowing out your hair, are you?" I look at Susan's wet, wavy head.

"Well, I—"

"No way. Then I'm leaving. I have Holocaust Lit with Maxx and I'm not going to be late."

"Testy, testy." She hunts in a basket for the right scunchii.

"I'm just telling you, this class is important. We don't have to walk together."

"You know"—she pulls on a woolly, fuchsia turtleneck that sufficiently hides a fading hickey—"you've changed."

"Changed since when?" I hear my voice crack.

Susan crams her Nutrition textbook into her leather backpack. "You've gotten . . . tough."

"Since when?"

"I don't know. Just lately."

I try to think about how I've changed. I don't feel tougher, and it's ironic that she says this now, after last night. I feel like I was so untough, like I folded. But in a sense I guess she's right, that in the past few days, I may not have stopped looking for distractions, but at least I know they're distractions, and that seems like a first step, a small one, but the beginning of stemming the tide and stopping myself from floating away.

Waiting for the elevator, I rummage for my cigarettes. I pull one out of the soft pack and stick it to my bottom lip. There's blood on the filter. My mouth is chapped from kissing Jake so much. I pat it where it's tender with the pads of my fingers.

"Mike's?" I ask outside, squinting and lighting my cigarette.

"Huh?" Susan waves showily at the smoke.

"Are we stopping at the truck?"

"Fine with me. You're Miss I-Have-to-Be-Early."

I ignore that. "Yeah, let's stop at the truck." I'm hungry. I want this ritual, something warm. We walk over the hill and past the bookstore. The sunlight makes shapes on the brick walk.

"Hey, Susan," calls a low male voice.

I put my hand up to shade my eyes. It's Topher Gant, one of the Phi Delt guys we hang out with. Probably asking Susan to another formal. She walks over to where he sits, lacing up his hiking boots on the steps of the house.

"I'll meet you at the truck," I call to Susan.

There's no line, which means we must be late for class. "Hi, Mike," I say.

"Hey, buddy. You look a little tired. You all right?" He puts my muffin on the grill for "toasting" and pours milk into my coffee.

"Yeah," I say softly. It sounds like a whispered croak. Somehow, just his asking if I'm all right has brought me to the verge of tears. I've never asked him if he's all right. I'm sure he has his own, more serious problems. I reach into my pocket for money.

He puts a lid on my coffee and organizes coffee, muffin, and napkin perfectly in the bag to avoid spillage. "Guy trouble?"

I can only nod my head and wonder how many girls stopping for muffins at the truck have guy problems.

"This one's on me. Don't let them get you down. It's not worth it. You're gonna go places, kid. You'll see."

"I guess so." I try to smile. But I can't imagine what places I'll actually go. I turn to leave and come face-to-face with Susan. "I thought you were—"

"Hanging out with Topher? I came to get you. What's this about your having guy problems?"

"I don't want to talk about it."

"I do." She shakes me by my shoulders.

"Ow."

"What's with you, Beck? What is going on?"

"Do you really want to know, Susan? Do you actually give a

shit about what's going on with me? Or do you want to know just enough to swoop in and make it all better?"

"What are you talking about? You don't tell us anything, Beck. You're out so late all the time. I hear all this crazy stuff. But nothing from you. I hear nothing from you."

"Because that wouldn't be fun. And we both know that I'm the fun one. I don't get to freak out. The second I get a little sad, like at the game, nobody can deal with it." Maybe I am toughening. My voice sounds strange to me, vibrating but firm, and I can't think of another time when I've talked to Susan this way, or even when we've had an argument more meaningful than Smokes vs. Palladium.

"Nobody can deal with it except Phoebe, right?" Susan says. "You are a fun person, Rebecca. And funny. And we do like that about you. But that doesn't mean you don't have the right to be sad. Maybe it'll just take a little getting used to, but don't just assume I can't handle it. It just worried me, at the game. The contrast was so dramatic."

We stand in the giant compass in the center of the Walk where it connects with Thirty-fourth Street. I feel like we're spinning. "Okay," I say. I try to start walking again but she holds me in place. She pulls me to her, tight, so my face is pressed into her hair. I smell her apple-pectin shampoo. The waves of hair muffle my sobs.

"I'm so sorry," she says. "Sometimes I do get sort of swept up in things around here. But I hope I haven't failed some kind of a test with you. Because you are my friend, even if you're sad. That means something to me." She pats my back lightly, again and again. I'm so tired, suddenly. I feel like a rag doll she's thrown over her shoulder. I almost want to go to sleep right here. Every sob drains me a little more. "It's okay. Just let it out."

Even though her class is in College Hall, just around the corner, she walks me all the way to Bennett Hall at the edge of campus. She gives me her Kleenex pocket pak. "I'll be home right after field hockey practice," she says. "Do you need anything?"

I shake my head.

"I'll go to Beijing," she says in a singsong voice meant to make me smile. It does.

"General Gau's chicken?" I say.

"You got it."

22
★
further complications

"Welcome," Maxx says as I walk in after class has begun.

"I'm sorry. I—"

"Don't worry about it. Chop, chop though. We need you in this discussion."

The chairs in the room are divided into two sections. Against the window is the main body of the class, with Annie Winger, the pudgy, miniskirted, blond Tri Delt, and J. P. Watson, the kicker for the football team, at the front. Against the other side of the room: Dan Miller—long sideburns, army pants—alone as usual. I look from side to side. Maxx often divides us according to our position on a certain text. But I missed the explanation about which side is which.

"So, Lowe," he says, "Primo Levi's depiction of the Holocaust, for all its dirty realness, is less effective than the heroic story of *Schindler's List*. If I had to teach just one of these books, I should teach *Schindler's List*—sit by the windows. Or, Levi's depiction is gritty and it's real and it's important. And, in fact, the characters in this book are heroic. Over there." He waves a hand in Dan's direction. "And, if, at any time, anyone wants to change position, just walk to the other side."

That's easy. I stride toward Dan.

"Hey," I say.

Dan pushes the chair beside him out just slightly in response.

"So, Primo Levi's book, *Survival in Auschwitz*. It's very dark. Depressing. Why read this thing?" Maxx says.

"I agree with you," Annie Winger says, as if Maxx is actually taking a position. "This stuff that they did in the book—taking their dead friends' fillings out to sell them, fighting each other over a piece of soap. I don't know if it really happened, but I don't want to hear it. There's a really important story, the story of the survival. People want to read that."

"So we should give people what they want," Maxx says.

"Well, like *Schindler's List*. That probably inspired some people. But the Levi book probably just made people more depressed."

"Interesting point," Maxx says. "When the topic is any old coming-of-age story, romance, whatever, we can afford to play around. With nonfiction about the Holocaust, too much is at stake. People need to be inspired. Neo-Nazism is alive and well, even today. We can't afford to have this Primo Levi message out there. Lowe?"

"The Primo Levi book *is* heroic and inspirational," I say. "In *Schindler's List,* a non-Jew sweeps in and becomes the reluctant hero. But Levi saves himself by the very acts we're now sitting back and criticizing in the light of our 1990s reasoning. We might not think we'd fight over a scrap of soap while we're sitting at the Palladium deciding what fraternity party to go to. But Levi is a hero because he did what he had to do, because he fought over the scrap of soap." In the momentary quiet J.P. walks over to me and Dan from the other side of the room, takes a seat. So I've changed his mind.

"So, Lowe, do you think you would have done it? Would you have been out there doing whatever it took to survive, even if it meant giving up the morality you had before?"

I think about last night. Should I have fought Jake off more? Could I have? Or was giving in actually the act of resistance? After all, I made it out of there. I'm still intact.

"I hope so," I say.

in bed with strangers

On the walk home from class, I bump into Phoebe. "Hey," she says. "You okay? Have you eaten?"

I shake my head.

"Want to go to Skolniks?"

I can't deal with the whole crowd there, swarming around. Plus, Jake might be there. I can't see Jake. "Somewhere less—"

"Out there? Sure, sure. You tell me."

"Let's go to Kelly's." I haven't been back there since the football game.

We walk for a while in silence. Phoebe keeps looking at me. I know she knows something's wrong. It's like that with Phoebe.

We get a back table by the window. I order French toast and bacon, as usual, and juice and coffee. I wonder what made me have to leave before. It seems so far away. Now I'm dying for the comfort of these things.

"I know you want to know what happened last night," I say.

"Honestly? Yeah, I'm wondering. You really seem, I don't know, a little shaken or something. But don't feel like you have to talk about it. You don't have to."

"We hooked up. I'm sorry. I'm so sorry."

"That's—wow. You don't have to be sorry. I'm not sure what to say."

"I didn't want to do it, but I did." I put my elbows on the table and cover my face with my hands.

Phoebe reaches over, pries my hands away gently, and looks at me. "Oh my god. Are you saying he—"

"He didn't rape me. Jake did not rape me. I didn't want to do it, but I let it happen because I wanted to get out of there and go home. And I really didn't want to have to walk alone. And I was kind of drunk." I bite my lip and stare out the window.

"He got you drunk?" Phoebe makes me look back.

"He gave me drinks and I drank them. Not many, but it was grain. And it was on top of what we'd had at the party. And on the way back to the house. But I'm the one who drank them. I got myself drunk."

"I'm so, so sorry." Phoebe pulls a stack of napkins from the metal box on the table and hands them to me, just as our food comes, steaming, to the table.

I dry my eyes. "It's okay."

"It's not, Beck."

"I know."

"What happened? How did it happen?"

"I don't know. I went back there, and we found the hat, and I was drinking, and things started. And I tried to stop them, but it just got hard to keep doing that—"

"More than once, you were trying to stop them?"

"Yeah—more than once. And then I just decided, just to get it over with. I shouldn't have given in. I mean, what was so scary about

213

the situation that I had to give in? Like I couldn't have gotten out of there? He's a Pi-O brother. C'mon." I try to laugh, but it sounds as fake as it feels.

"Everything about that situation is scary," Phoebe says. "It's late at night. You've had too much to drink. Jake's not a small guy. You want to get out of there. You don't want him to be mad at you."

"The thing I was most scared of was that if I didn't sleep with him, he wasn't going to walk me home. So I did it with him and I walked home alone anyway." I cut my French toast into squares but I can't make myself eat one.

"I never should have let you go," Phoebe says.

"What are you talking about?"

"I let you leave Wawa with him."

"Phoebe, please, it wasn't your fault. If anything I feel guilty for letting anything happen with someone you liked."

"Oh, God, please. I drag you to the party, I introduce you to Jake, then I let you leave Wawa with him, drunk, knowing you're going back to the house."

"Phoebe, I wasn't even really drunk when I left Wawa. I drank when I got there, and on the way. Plus I wanted the hat right that second. I was so worried about losing it. It just—it means something to me." I play back the events yet another time, think how I could have done it differently. Even if I had to have the hat that night, I could have said no to the drinks. I could have waited downstairs for Jake. I could have kept saying no and just walked myself home, earlier and without this violation. There's something I keep looking for in these one-night interactions, and I wonder if I'll ever stop looking, even now.

Phoebe eats in silence, watching me pour the syrup, slowly and evenly, along the cracks between the toast pieces, still eating nothing.

"It's happened to me too," Phoebe says finally.

"What do you mean?"

"Where the lines are kind of gray. With Chevs."

"What do you mean, with Chevs?"

"A few weeks before we broke up. He was wasted. I was planning on staying over there, but I just didn't want to be around him, he was being such a pig. He reeked, and he was all over me, and he was like a totally different person. And I just did it with him. Because it would be easier than having him bug me and be all over me all night. And he was scary and out of control. I don't know. I felt so bad afterward. He actually pissed on himself in the bed. It was like being with a complete stranger. I sat there and cried for an hour when it was over and he never even heard me."

"God, that's horrible. Why didn't you ever tell me?"

"Because I thought I was weak. To do it with that slimeball. And to complain about it. So I felt like I was forced to sleep with my ex-boyfriend. Big deal. You're not eating."

"It is a big deal, Phoebe."

"I know it's different than with you. But even though it was Chevs, it really wasn't Chevs. I really was scared of what would happen if I said no to him. He was just—rough—all of a sudden."

I watch Phoebe watching something outside the window, far away.

24

★

number 6 picks it up

Everyone is waiting for me when I get home. It's like one of those interventions you see on TV, like when the gang on *90210* tells Luke Perry he's a drug addict after he wrecks his Porsche driving too fast in the canyons. I wonder if I am Dylan tonight. "Hi, guys," I say, dropping my book bag on a chair. "What's going on?"

"Nothing. I just thought it would be nice if we all ate together. We haven't done that in a while," Susan says.

"Not since you were on Jane's ridiculous health kick and you made us all sit around eating steamed vegetables all night," Maggie says.

"They're full of nutrients," Jane squeaks.

"When I look at you, I actually *see* broccoli," says Maggie. "You're like a tiny broccoli spear in leggings."

"Hey," Jane wails, frowning.

"Okay, okay, stop," I say. "So what time's dinner?"

"Six," Susan says.

"I've got work to do," I say. "I'm going to Steinberg-Deitrich until then, okay?"

"But afterwards, you'll come home?" Susan says.

"Yes. I'll come home." I start packing books into my bag. I'm way behind in Art History and I don't want to face Ms. Slater again without reading. Plus I have more pages due in *Moby Dick*.

I get a teacher's desk at Steinberg-Deitrich and lay out all my stuff. There's a group of big guys in the back. I recognize Bill, this football player I knew freshman year. He was really good at calculus and people used to line up outside his room for help. He tips his baseball hat and mouths "Hey."

I smile back. Then I motion for him to come over.

"Hey, you," he says, "what's up? Haven't seen you in a while."

"I'm okay."

"Are you still seeing that little guy in Sigma Chi?"

Everyone is little to Bill. Scott Childs is five feet ten. "No. Are you still with that skinny track girl?"

"Ha ha. Yeah. Actually, I pinned her last week."

"You pinned her?"

"At the fraternity. You knew I was in FIJI, right?"

"Oh, yeah. So it's like a pre-engagement?"

"Pretty much."

I can't believe how calm he is about all this. So there actually are some guys who will freely use a word like *engagement* to describe their relationship.

"Do you still play football?"

"Yeah." He laughs. "You don't go to games?"

"I go to every game. I guess I'm just never paying that much attention."

"That's nice. Thank you."

"Sorry. I didn't mean it like that. Hey—do you know Number Six?"

"On the team? Yeah, of course I do. That's Pitzer. Right over there."

Pitzer is big, like the others, with four-foot shoulders, dark, short hair trimmed in a style like Wally on *Leave It to Beaver.* His face looks soft, but handsome, though not in a *GQ* kind of way. Susan would call him dumb looking, but I don't think so. I've never thought football players were dumb since the only one I've known is Bill and he's so good at calculus. "That's Number Six?"

"Living and breathing," Bill says. "So you don't know I'm playing this year, but you know Pit. Nice."

"He lets you call him Pit?"

"Yeah, why not? You got the hots for him or something?"

"No, I—"

"He's a good guy. You got good taste. Yo, Pit, c'mere."

"Stop! What are you doing?"

But it's too late. Number Six is walking toward the front of the room, and Bill, of course, is walking away. Pit leans down over the desk and whispers, "Hi. What's going on? Is this about Art History? Because that's not my best subject. I'm pulling a B-minus."

I hear sputtering from the rows of players.

"You take Art History?" I ask.

He bends his knees and squats down beside my chair so he's at my eye level. "Yeah. You've never seen me?"

"Uh, no. But I don't have a question about Art History. I wanted to ask you about the game." I can't believe I'm doing it. I can't even frame what it is I want to know.

"About the game?"

"Yeah. Not to be . . . Please don't take this . . . About the game where you fumbled the ball." I want him to read me, to know I'm not a bad person, that there's just something I just need to know. I want him to have an instinct about me, to see where I'm going and where I've been, to know what this means to me.

"Jesus, you really have a way with people. What are you, with he newspaper or something? It's not a big deal. So I fumbled the ball." He looks at me, shakes his head, and gets up.

"Wait—that's not—I didn't mean—" I grab his hand but he shakes it free. I realize how stupid it was, to think this stranger would have some kind of instinct about me, when the one thing I've started to realize is that I barely have the right instincts about myself.

"I've got work to do," he says. "Ellsworth Kelly paper."

Only we don't have a paper due this week. He doesn't go back to his desk. He keeps walking, pushes open the door to the room. The other players look up. I follow him.

"Wait, wait!" I yell. People look up from their work, and a few of them shush me angrily. "Pitzer!"

He keeps walking. "Look," he says finally, turning back to me for a split second, "I'm not mad at you or anything. I just don't want to talk about it."

"But—" We're at the outside door now, by the grape arbor vines where I fell apart before. "Just wait one second. Pit."

"It's Jonah."

"Okay, Jonah. I'm sorry. I just—you have to understand that after the game I went a little—I don't know, crazy or something."

"You went crazy? Because I fumbled the ball?" He rolls his eyes.

"I didn't go crazy because you fumbled the ball. Well, I did, actually, but not in the way you think. I just went crazy wondering what you were feeling when you fumbled the ball, when they said your name like that, out loud, telling everyone that it was your fault—"

"Yeah, yeah. I remember. You want to know how I felt? Why? Is this for a psych paper or something?"

"No. I just—" There has to be a way for me to make him understand. I don't even care about blurting out my feelings to someone I don't know. I just want him to know me. I want him to see that we have this connection, and I have to know if he's okay, if he recovered after he fumbled the ball, if I'll recover. "Do you sometimes feel like you just can't stop thinking about everything? Like there was a time when you could stop, when you were little or something. Or when you were at a party, drinking and just dancing like a maniac. And then it's like you have to just keep going from forgetting to forgetting because if you actually have to sit down and think about things it's too much? The people counting on you. And your parents telling you all the ways they failed, like you have to make up for every one. And people who only like you when you're funny and when you've got the best plan and the late-night invites to Zete and you just feel like everything is so conditional and you just can't afford to drop the ball, but it's like your hands are buttered and everything is just slipping all of the time, and—"

"I think you're a little bit crazy," Jonah says, handing me a hankie from his pocket.

I take it, dab the corners of my eyes. "I know."

"It sucks to fumble. And you're out there and everyone's watching and you're making crazy girls in the stands have these weird breakdowns."

We both laugh.

"But you have to think of the big picture," he says. "It's not the last screwup. Everybody screws up. All the time. Maybe the coach is gonna ream you. But he'll get over it. Isn't it kind of comforting in a way? Because that's pretty much the worst that can happen. You let something slip. And then the world does not fall apart. And your little brother still wants to be just like you. Know what I mean?"

"Sort of. I've just never let something slip."

"Wow."

"Maybe I should try it."

"You don't have to try it. You can just know that it'll probably happen, and if it does, you'll still be the same person."

"You say that now, but this game wasn't so important. What if you pull a Bill Buckner in the play-offs against Cornell?"

"Ouch. What are you trying to do, jinx me?"

"You didn't answer my question."

"Someone loves even Bill Buckner," he says.

25
★
pulling away from the island

I am home just in time for supper. Susan slides across the room on her sock feet, bangs her palm against the metal closet to stop, and opens the door just as I'm turning the handle. "Hey, you," she says. "How are you doing?"

"Okay. Hungry."

Maggie and Jane are already eating. Maggie picks at the remains of the General Gau coating on the bottom of a take-out box, and Jane's dumped her usual large order of steamed white rice into a bowl and is removing a Tupperware container full of broccoli crowns from the microwave. Maggie stops picking to hand me three white boxes on a paper plate.

"So," Jane says, walking over and banging her fist on the table, "table talk!"

Maggie bangs her fist too. Susan looks at me.

"I want to know where Rebecca Lowe was last night. I know I got in at three, and there was no sign," Jane says. "Is the mysterious Trey back in the picture? Or Scott Childs? Or the freshman? It's so hard to keep up."

"Give her a break," Susan says. "Let her eat her food."

* * *

After we eat, Susan voluntarily cleans up. "I'm taking care of it," she says, pulling my plate from my hand. Then she begs me to go to Smokes for Sink or Swim.

"I don't know," I say. "I'm really tired."

Jane and Maggie look at each other.

"Oh, c'mon," Susan says, "you'll wake up when you get there."

I shoot her a quick look.

"You're right," she says. "You're right. Smokes will always be there. Get your rest."

"Let me go lie down for a while and I'll see how I feel."

They're quiet until I walk into my room. As soon as I close the door, though, I can hear them whispering. I wonder if they're planning to have me committed or something. It's nice, though, that they're worrying. Jane and Susan need to worry once in a while. I lie on my bed and try not to think about Jake, and then Ryan. Eventually, I fall asleep, even with the thoughts of the conversation with Jonah and what it all means zipping along under the screen of my eyelids.

When I wake up, Maggie's back at the library and Susan and Jane are just getting ready to go to Smokes. I decide to go too. I don't feel like staying here alone with all of my thoughts. And I can't sleep anymore.

We all crowd into Jane and Susan's room to pick clothes. I settle on my best-fitting jeans, a light purple oxford with a camisole showing under it, and my black boots. With a tiny brush, I carefully apply mauve glaze lip gloss. I peer into the corner of Susan's cosmetic mirror. It's the Clairol kind some of my friends had in high school, bordered with small round bulbs like mirrors in Vegas showgirl dressing rooms. You can change how bright the light is by turning the dial to different settings: Day, Evening, Night. Wouldn't it be amazing, I imagine for a minute, if the settings said Strong and Unafraid, Be Someone Else for a Little While, and Rosy Jolt of Confidence.

227

"What do you see?" Susan asks, watching me.

But I'm not even sure. "I'm starting to get unibrow," I say.

"You can borrow my tweezers," Jane says.

But Susan just looks at me. I know she knows I've avoided the answer.

"You look pretty," she says.

I guess maybe I do.

Susan and Jane fight over who gets to wear the purple J Crew turtleneck. They each have one but don't want to be twins. We run to Smokes without our coats.

The line snakes along the side of several storefronts as usual. Nate is there. He's all excited because he just got a VIP card.

"You look good, kid," he says, poking me in the side and making me laugh. "What's up?" He nods at Susan, giving her a decently concealed once-over.

"I'm not a kid, Nate."

He's taken aback for a second. "You're right. I should stop calling you that. So, you guys want to horn in on my VIP action?"

Susan and I laugh. The VIP pass costs $50 and gives you the privilege to cut in line.

"No," I say. "Let's just wait in line." I turn to Susan. "It's okay out here."

She shrugs. I see her wave away the Drexel bouncer, who's come out to show us to the short line.

Inside, I see Phoebe and instantly smile. "Back again," she says. "How are you doing?"

"I'm okay. I won't stay long. Kind of just wanted to see if I could do it."

"Do what?"

"Go out, have fun without getting completely smashed, without

228

hooking up with some random. Go out and be in the world without needing . . . I don't know. Something more. Something numbing."

"That seems like a good idea."

"Yeah." I look around and fidget with an imaginary straw and a glass, wishing I had brought cigarettes.

"How's it going so far?" Phoebe asks, watching me play with a loose thread on the edge of my sweater.

"I feel incredibly tense. I desperately want vodka, and everyone around here seems really stupid. Is this why I have to drag you out half the time?" I ask, watching a blonde across the room giggle and toss her ponytail from side to side while a PIKA pledge probably recites some line from *Fletch*.

"Bingo," Phoebe says.

"Wow, I totally empathize. I'm sorry," I say.

"So how are you doing? You didn't answer me before. About what happened with Jake." She guides me to a ledge that we can lean on around the booths by the bar.

"I'm doing okay. Maybe I haven't really thought about it enough yet, though. Is that what you're supposed to do, go off to some deserted place or something and sit around and really think about things and what they all mean? Because I never do that. I go to classes and dance at parties and get bagels at Skolniks."

"I think you do something in between," Phoebe says. "You don't go to an island. But you don't run off to Sigma Chi every time you want to not think about something."

"I know you're right. Speaking of things I don't want to think about . . ."

"Ryan never called."

"Yeah," I say. "My life is so predictable. I am such a fucking idiot. I gave him a book. Why did I do that? He probably doesn't even read."

"He probably does read."

"I know."

"He's not horrible. He's got a lot of things going for him. I can totally see why you fell for him. He's tall. He's handsome. He's smart. He's even Jewish. He said all of these things to you and you had no reason not to believe him. You had every reason to want to believe him, actually."

"Maybe the first time," I say.

"Every time. I can't blame you for hoping about this. No one would. And no one would blame you for giving him another chance. We just do that. It's like we're programmed to. It takes about a million chances to finally face it. You think there weren't warning signs with Chevs? I ignored them. I just didn't want my life not to be organized around—this boyfriend. You want to not think the worst, because you gave something to this person. A piece of you. You let go."

"I feel like such an ass." I rest my elbow on the wooden ledge, put my hand on my head, and sigh.

"He's the ass," Phoebe says, putting her drink down on the ledge so hard that some drops flick onto the wood. "Seriously, don't blame yourself, okay? The way you trust people is a good quality about you. So he comes in and fucks with that, that's his problem. You're human! You liked Ryan. You lost your virginity to him. And he keeps making all these excuses and saying all the right things, so it feels like it's unfinished business with him. It'll take time, believe me, I know. Remember how devastated I was about Chevs? Well, I slept with him again, even after everything he did. I thought we were starting something again, but it turns out he just thought we could still sleep together, as friends, until we met other people."

"What a jerk. I never knew that."

"Yeah, that's because it's pretty fucking humiliating. The point is that we all do things we're not so proud of sometimes. It takes a while to get someone out of your system. I think you kind of have to hit rock bottom."

"God, I can't imagine getting more rock than this. So, after rock bottom, then what? When will I stop thinking about Ryan?"

"Completely? Maybe never. But he'll get smaller and smaller, like he's on an island and you're on a boat speeding away. It just takes time. You haven't had any time yet."

"Is he stranded on the island?" I ask hopefully.

Then Jane taps me on the shoulder. "Hi, Phoebe," she says. "We're going downstairs, Beck. Susan wants to carve her name in a booth all of a sudden. Want to come?"

"No thanks," I say, "I think we'll hang out up here."

Jane disappears into a throng of people, shrugging her shoulders.

"You know where we haven't been in a while?" Phoebe asks. "Billybob's. Let's blow this pop stand and go have a calorie fest. My treat." Phoebe grabs my arm and leads me through the crowd. At the bottom of the stairs, she stops dead in her tracks. "Shit," she says, leaning back to whisper in my ear. "It's Ryan. Do you want to go back?"

"Hell no." I am not going to be afraid. I am not going to rearrange my life just because of him this time. I won't give him the satisfaction.

"Hey," he says coolly, motioning for his friends to go ahead up the stairs.

"Is there anything you want to say to me?" I ask.

"Nope." Then: "Oh, yeah, thanks for the book."

"Thanks for the book? That's it?"

"Whatever. What do you want me to say?" He yells toward the stairs, "Yo, Carter! Order me a Bud!"

I pull Phoebe's arm, and we start walking out. But at the door, she turns around. "Wait a minute," she says. "Let's just not let him get away with this." She opens the door back up and we catch him at the top of the stairs. "Hold on," Phoebe says, grabbing his sleeve. "You arrogant underage fuck. She is the best thing that ever slipped through your fingers. Have a nice life working at Morgan Stanley and doing it missionary style on Saturday nights with your dumb, unimaginative, fake-titted bimbo wife."

Ryan stands there, arms dropped at his sides, mouth hanging open.

I look him in the eyes. "It's so sad, Ryan," I say, my voice low.

He just stares at me.

"Do you have so many wonderful relationships in your life? Can you really afford to be so dismissive? Of someone like me?" *Someone real,* I think.

He just stands there, still staring.

"God, Ryan, I feel so sorry for you," I say, shaking my head. I back away a few steps, leaving him standing there, and then I grab Phoebe's hand again, and we run back out onto the sidewalk. "'Fake-titted bimbo wife?'" I say. We laugh all the way to Billybob's. We order chicken cheese steaks and cheese fries.

"What are you guys so happy about?" asks the man behind the counter, scraping the grease out to the edge of the grill.

"What's to be unhappy about?" Phoebe says.

"Well, all right," he says.

26

★

lost and finding

Phoebe calls in the morning, which is odd because neither of us has a class. "What's going on?" I mumble into the phone.

"Sorry to wake you," she says, sounding oddly perky, "but I've got an idea. What are you doing this morning?"

"Sleeping. Reading. Why? What's up?"

"I thought we could declare our majors."

"What? Today? Why?"

"Why not? I have an appointment with Old Guy, what's his face, the head of the department. You can go in after me, I'm sure. I have a half an hour. How long does it take to declare yourself an English major?"

"Why now?"

"Why not now? Remember you always said you didn't want to end up one of those people who never declares and then has to take some ridiculous class to graduate. Come with me."

"What's your concentration?"

"Brit Lit. What's yours?"

"That's kind of the thing. I've taken a lot of the right classes, but I don't like any of the concentrations. I was planning to develop my own concentration. It would be, like, the literature of blacks, Jews, and women. Literature of outsiders."

"So ask him! Why the hell couldn't you? That sounds amazing."

Phoebe picks me up outside my high-rise and hands me a frosted chocolate Pop-Tart.

"Thanks. Do we have time for the truck? I'm massively in need of caffeine."

"Definitely," Phoebe says.

"Hey, kid," Mike says. "The usual?"

"Just two coffees, please. Skim milk and Sweet 'n Low."

"And how's the boy situation today?" he asks, pressing the lids onto the paper cups.

"Better." I'm actually, given the hour, in a pretty good mood. Phoebe looks at me, but I don't feel like explaining.

"Good. Don't let the turkeys get you down," Mike says. "'Cause at the end of the day, they're just turkeys."

"I won't," I say, taking the coffees and passing Phoebe hers. "And thank you."

Phoebe comes out of her meeting smiling. "No problem. He's in a good mood. And it's just one thing to cross off your to-do list."

"Wish me luck." I knock lightly on the door.

"Ms. Lowe, come on in. Are you also declaring with a British Literature concentration?"

"Not exactly. I've kind of been designing my own concentration, so I was hoping to declare that today. It's about the literature of blacks, Jews, and women. I want to call it Voices of Outsiders." I

235

hand him the scribbled list of courses I've taken and plan to take.

"The thing is," he says, raising his eyebrows and tilting back in a wing chair not meant to tilt, "that, while your idea is interesting, and while I commend your taking these classes, what you propose is not necessarily scholarly. We prefer, and this is the way that the concentrations are set up, that you get a real depth in one particular time period or form."

"But I don't understand why what I'm suggesting is not scholarly."

He looks up from under his bifocals and says nothing.

"I mean, for the English-major part, I'm still going to have to read Milton and all that anyway. So I will have the classical background. You can see from my transcript that I already took Brit Lit One. And got an A in it. And in History of the Novel with Professor Maxx too. Since the school offers all of these classes on blacks, Jews, and women, how can you then turn around and say those classes are somehow less valid, or not valid at all? It's judgmental. It's actually discriminatory. Not to be rude. It just doesn't make sense."

He fingers the edge of a brown leather planner. In the pause I try to imagine what I'll do if this doesn't work out. But I can't.

"But the concentrations, by allowing you to focus deeply, broadly, on a particular time period, or on a particular type of literature over a span of time, help assure that your scholarship is layered, connected," he says.

I try to marshal the right words. I will make this a reality. I'm not going to sit back and let him wrap me in more red tape. I know what I want now. "But the connection is in the focus on outsiders. Which is a major focus in literature. The link is the experience of marginalization. And I can't see how you could say that there's not breadth there, or layers."

After a long pause, he says, "I'll take it under advisement."

"You mean you can't tell me now? But I really need to know this. If I can't use any of these classes toward my concentration, I may have a hard time fulfilling my concentration, plus all of the other requirements—"

"Patience, Ms. Lowe. We'll see what we can do."

"I am trying to do something here that's important."

"I hear you, Ms. Lowe. I'll be in touch."

I mutter some thank-yous but they get lost in the action of my slamming things into my book bag, slapping it shut, and throwing it over my shoulder so hard that I almost lose my balance.

Phoebe is waiting for me in the hallway. "Ooooh—that good, huh?" she says when she sees my face.

"He'll take it 'under advisement.'"

"At least you tried, though. And maybe it'll work out. You have to wait and see."

"I hate to wait and see." I sigh, knowing, at the same time, that before Phoebe called this morning I wasn't even worrying about this at all. It's probably not the end of the world.

The phone is ringing as I turn my key in the lock. I grab it on the last ring.

"Yeah?"

"Is it really you?" This is how my mother likes to begin a phone conversation. She's telling me how hard I am to reach.

"Yep. What's up?"

"You sound angry or something." Her own voice has shifted into something else too.

"Mom, it's just that I'm having some problems with school."

"With grades?"

"No, not with grades!" I throw my book bag against the wall and watch some papers break free from my spiral and flutter to the floor.

"You know what? I don't need to be talked to like this."

"Did you just call me to ask about my grades and to yell at me?"

Then no one says anything.

"God, Rebecca, we are just not getting along."

It's not a news flash, but neither of us has ever just said this flat out before. She sounds like she's crying now.

"Nope, Mom, we really aren't."

"It's just been a tough year for us. A tough few years, hasn't it?"

"Yeah, it has." Now I'm crying too.

"Well, maybe it will get better."

"Yeah, Mom. Maybe it will."

I hang up the phone and look at the two old pictures taped to the bottom edge of my quote wall. One is of my father, in the hat, standing in front of his Thunderbird. The other is a picture of my mom, when she was in graduate school. Her hair is dark and smooth, long and parted in the middle. She wears a big silver necklace with a green stone that lies in the nest of her collarbones. She's sitting, and the camera has caught her by surprise. But she is smiling. My mother is smiling.

let the choir sing

"You're home," says Susan, while my key's still in the lock. It's late, but now that it's spring, it's still lightish out. I like that; it makes it seem like more is always possible.

"Yeah. Why are you looking at me like you're afraid of something."

"I'm not. I just—there's a phone message for you."

I look up. I know who I want it to be before I can stop myself from wanting. It's been months.

"Ryan called."

"Oh?" I know my fake-casual tone is completely transparent. My stomach churns. "What did he say?"

"He sounded like he was completely wasted. There was some kind of game on TV in the background."

"Susan, what did he say?"

"I saved the message." She gestures at the machine.

I stand there too long, my finger hovering over the button. Susan walks out into her room.

"Yo, Beck. What's up? Jared and I are at New Deck. Thought you might want to come over. For old times' sake or whatever. We're drinking vodka shots, kind of in your honor, and . . ." The message cuts out, then picks up again.

"Rebecca, it's Jared. Ryan's very fucked up and he somehow has convinced himself that you're going to give him the time of day. Look, he knows you're really cool and he's sorry he fucked it all up with you. Maybe you could give him another chance . . ."

Ryan's slurry voice comes back. "Come over! Seriously. I—I told my mother about you. We just, I think we could have been, we could be—let's just talk. Seriously. Come over. We're at New Deck. Bye."

I know that Susan's in her room worrying that I'm going to gloss up my lips and take off for New Deck. And in spite of everything I still feel some butterflies of wanting, my heart rising up a little. It's so amazing to me still, how even after everything he's done, even though I see through him, even though I'm smart, how my intelligence completely fails me over and over with guys, how something else gets behind the wheel and starts driving right over me. God, his voice—deep and distinctive and assured, even though he's drunk; it seems to reach a place in me I forgot I could even get to. And he sounds like there's some nugget of truth there and maybe—

But I'm too tired today. Too tired to wear tight clothes and make-up, too tired to make good comebacks, swallow bitter shots, wonder what will happen next. Or maybe today I'm not tired enough.

The sky is the color of nighttime in children's books. I walk down the hall to my room.

"Beck, are you okay? Where are you going?"

I change into running tights, lace up my sneakers, click my Madonna tape into my Walkman.

"You're going running?" Susan asks as I brush past. "Now? I thought we'd—"

I look back at her.

"Okay," she says. She watches me go.

I stretch outside, reaching as high as I can and then folding my body in half and hanging, looking at everything upside down.

Running always feels a little strange to me at first, like my body wasn't meant to move that way. I push up the hill that Susan and I walked down on the day of the game, over the bridge and past the bookstore, then ease down, cranking up my Walkman. Madonna's voice in my ears, I find my rhythm. And then I truly begin. I run hard. Madonna kicks into "Like a Prayer." The air is cold in my face. I run like I'm breaking through a ribbon at the end of a marathon with every single step. "When you call my name, it's like a little prayer . . ." Pound. Pound. Pound. Past Steinberg-Deitrich, where I first met Number Six, and the Palladium, where lights blaze through the Gothic windows, across Thirty-fourth Street to Bennett Hall. I love this school. My lungs feel like they're bleeding. I smile through it.

I feel pretty when I run, even without makeup: flushed, glistening, muscular. I feel strong, noticing my breath as I exhale, pumping my arms with each stride. I feel the muscles in my thighs and calves propelling me forward. I want to keep going. And so what if I fumble? Number Six is okay. I saw him in Filmmaking today. He smiled at me.

Like this is the only one . . .

Floating
Robin Troy

The Perks of Being a Wallflower
Stephen Chbosky

The Fuck-up
Arthur Nersesian

Dreamworld
Jane Goldman

Fake Liar Cheat
Tod Goldberg

Pieces
edited by Stephen Chbosky

Dogrun
Arthur Nersesian

Brave New Girl
Louisa Luna

The Foreigner
Meg Castaldo

Tunnel Vision
Keith Lowe

More from the young, the hip, and the up-and-coming. Brought to you by MTV Books.